for Liza!

Dirk Quigby's Guide To
THE AFTERLIFE

love

EE King

An E.A.P. Fairy Tale for Adults of All Ages

At Exterminating Angel Press,
we're taking a new approach to our
world. A new way of looking at things.
New stories, new ways to live our lives.
We're dreaming how we want our lives
and our world to be...

Also from
Exterminating Angel Press

3 Dead Princes:
An Anarchist Fairy Tale
by Danbert Nobacon
Illustrated by Alex Cox

Jam Today:*A Diary of Cooking
With What You've Got*
by Tod Davies

Correcting Jesus: *2000 Years of
Changing the Story*
by Brian Griffith

The Supergirls: *Fashion, Feminism,
Fantasy, and the History of
Comic Book Heroines*
by Mike Madrid

Dirk Quigby's
GUIDE TO THE
AFTERLIFE

All You
Need To Know
To Choose the Right
Heaven
Plus
A Five-Star Rating System
for Music, Food, Drink,
& Accommodations

E.E. KING

EXTERMINATING ANGEL
PRESS

Portions of this book first appeared, some in different form, on the
Exterminating Angel Press online magazine at
www.exterminatingangel.com

EXTERMINATING ANGEL PRESS
"Creative Solutions for Practical Idealists"
Visit **www.exterminatingangel.com** to join the conversation
info@exterminatingangel.com

Book design by Mike Madrid

King, E. E., 1959-
    Dirk Quigby's guide to the afterlife : all you need to know to choose
the right heaven : plus a five-star rating system for music, food, drink,
& accommodations / E.E. King.
    p. cm.
    ISBN 978-1-935259-08-4 (alk. paper) -- ISBN 978-1-935259-11-4
(electronic book text)
    1. Future life--Fiction. 2. Travel writers--Fiction. I. Title.
PS3611.I5759D57 2010
813'.6--dc22

                                    2010016250

Printed in The United States of America
Ashland, Oregon

A Handy Guide to the Heavens
of Dirk Quigby's Guide

This book is dedicated to my wonderful witty mother, for her endless belief, support, and editorial acumen.
And to Kevan King, who was subjected to endless renditions of Dirk, and provided many of the humorous anecdotes and lines for this tale.
Anything you don't like is his idea.

All biological info., religious beliefs, and recipes are based on fact.
Author Dirk Quigby's comments are in italics.

This book intends no disrespect toward any persons of a true and abiding faith.

On the other hand, it intends no respect either.

In the Beginning

This is the tale of the short happy life of Dirk Quigby. The time is perilously close to the present, or to be more precise, next Tuesday. Next Tuesday, which was to arrive a week after last Tuesday, our hero had saved a cat. It was a neighbor's cat, trapped in a storm drain due to inquisitiveness and irresponsibility.

Dirk, a tall, lanky, slightly stooped man in his early forties, had angled his long form into the drain, grabbed the cat by the scruff of its neck, and heaved upward. The cat was not particularly appreciative. It scratched Dirk's face and leapt out of his arms. Once on solid ground, it turned and slowly blinked one of its blue-green eyes before departing.

A thin trickle of blood dripped onto Dirk's full lips, which would have been sensuous had they not been tightened and pursed. His brown soulful eyes were sad. The only feature of Dirk's that never appeared vanquished was his thick, glossy brown hair. But this was due to genetics rather than grooming. Dirk's mother, Lulu, had been a wild beauty. At nineteen, pregnant with Dirk, she had briefly married, the union lasting just long enough for her to conceive Dirk's sister, Mary.

The departure of Dirk's father was followed by a string of boyfriends, some who liked children, some who did not. Most didn't stay around long enough to make much of an impact.

Dirk had longed for a loving father, if not on Earth, then in Heaven. He wanted to confide his troubles to someone and be comforted.

As Dirk grew up, he dreamed of traveling to distant lands, chronicling diverse cultures and mysterious peoples. He would build bridges with words and foster understanding with his pen. But first, he needed some actual travel experience.

At twenty-two, he took a job with the advertising firm of Pesky, Pesky, & Pesky, Inc. He planned to build up a small nest egg, and then take off. However, the years passed and Dirk remained stuck to his desk—a nine-to-five slave in an airless cell, trapped, it seemed, until retirement. He toiled without joy and for scant salary, trying to make people covet the uncovetable by furnishing producers with snappy, often salacious sales slogans. He was held captive by fear and his 401(k) plan, ensnared in a pair of golden (or more accurately, bronze or perhaps tin) handcuffs. A dream of security kept him chained to nowhere.

He was designed for better things. He must be, else what was the point of life? Laboring to convince fat women that the "Jell-O Diet Plan" would make them thin? That Macho Beer would gain an ugly man the attention of beautiful babes?

The fat and the ugly would both soon be the quick and the dead, Dirk reasoned. Their weight and repulsiveness of no more import than passing litheness and loveliness. There must be a greater purpose. There must be more to life than … life.

Of course, Dirk realized he was hardly the first to find the ephemera of reality disheartening. Even Neanderthals put flowers in the graves of their dead.

Dirk looked for meaning in life, and finding none, or at least no unified-meaning theory, considered the afterlife.

After all, if a tree falls in the forest and I don't hear it, who cares?

Dirk felt like a chimp trying to understand NASA. Who could offer a cogent rationale for a tsunami, or explain why one baby was born in Africa, to starve, suffer, and die, while another baby was born Paris Hilton, to diet, party, and pose naked? There are those who claim that we choose our own existence … but then, who wouldn't choose to be

Paris Hilton—and why did Paris Hilton get to be Paris Hilton? Wouldn't Gandhi have made a more deserving Paris Hilton?

People are born beautiful, brilliant, talented … or lucky. Was luck a gene? Paris Hilton, Ringo Starr, lottery winners … they all got the luck gene.

If there was an answer, it must be in the afterlife. Ah, the afterlife: therein lay both solution and conundrum. The only creed religions seemed to agree on was that they were the Way, the Light, the Truth. Only followers of their own religion went to Heaven, and everyone else was damned. How was Dirk supposed to make an educated choice?

Ask and It Shall Be Given

I'd like to believe in the terrible truth, in the beautiful lie.
—Neil and Tim Finn

Dirk entered his cheerless apartment. His décor, such as it was, had been unchanged for years, frozen in time. He had not planned to be there long; it was meant to be a small way-station before the start of life's journey. The rooms were decorated with ragged travel posters and a few faded Rousseau jungles from his college days. Though aged and weathered, his apartment still possessed the dreams and wanderlust that Dirk had lost.

With a poignant sigh, Dirk grabbed a beer and slumped onto his overstuffed couch. He listlessly punched the remote control on his television. The TV, which usually required a good two minutes of snow and static before showing a fuzzy picture, snapped sharply into focus. The picture was clear, the color bright.

This was especially surprising because Dirk Quigby had a black-and-white TV.

Gazing intently into Dirk's eyes was a darkly handsome man. He was tan, with glossy raven hair, deep-set brilliant black eyes, and even features. Dirk wondered if it was a Cary Grant Classics night. "Are you concerned about your future?" Cary asked in the sympathetic voice used by newscasters and psychics.

Dirk nodded.

"Do you feel like you're missing something?"

Dirk inclined his head in agreement.

"Do you feel there must be more to life than life? Do you wonder about the afterlife?"

Dirk had disregarded the colorful transformation of his hitherto black-and-white set, but now he snapped to attention.

Why am I talking to Cary Grant, Dirk thought. *And why is Cary Grant making an infomercial?*

Still, Dirk had been in the ad business a long, long time—far too long to be suckered into something just because Cary Grant appeared to be addressing his recent thoughts.

"We are now offering," the Cary look-alike continued, "a fully accredited course to provide you with the answers to just such questions.

"World Religion and Afterlife 101 is a brief yet comprehensive guide to all the world's major religions, with special emphasis on Afterlife and Heaven. Enroll now and all this knowledge can be yours (*Here it comes,* Dirk thought) for the amazing, incredible, phenomenally low, low, lowwww price of fifteen dollars."

Fifteen dollars, that is low. Too low.

"Lest you fear the price is too low, be aware that this is a One-Time Offer only! After tonight, the price will return to its normal $575."

Whew, quite a difference. Why?

"Quite a difference, eh? Why, you may ask … why are we offering such a low, low, lowww price tonight? Knowledge, my friends! We want to encourage the quest for knowledge!"

I'll bet. You want to encourage the quest for more money in your pocket.

"Skeptical? If not completely satisfied with the knowledge you receive, we will offer a ten-day, one hundred percent, money-back guarantee. Simply call 1-666-IHEAVEN … that's 1-666-443-2836, to reserve your space tonight!"

What have I got to lose? It's only fifteen dollars.

"After all, what have you got to lose … except your ignorance? Register on-line at www.whatsafterlife.com. That's www.whatsafterlife .com."

Suddenly the color flashed off, replaced by the usual black-and-white static and snow.

Geez, that's some connection! They must have a really powerful signal.

Dirk slouched over to his laptop. Even before he finished typing www.w, "Welcome Dirk," blazed onto the screen.

Computers are amazing! I didn't even log in.

"Do you wonder about the meaning of life, or even if there is a meaning?"

Yes.

"Well, wonder no longer. Instead, take advantage of our *amazing introductory offer*. No, that's NO money down. Simply press the YES button flashing NOW. You'll receive all material absolutely free, a $560 saving. And, as a *Special incentive*, this Thursday only, an *exceptionally* qualified instructor will be available to answer all your questions."

That's tomorrow, there's no way I can receive anything by then. Nevertheless, almost without volition, Dirk clicked "yes."

Congratulations! We'll see you tomorrow, 8 PM, at Elysium College!

I've never heard of Elysium College.

"Need a map?"

A map appeared on the screen.

It's right around the corner. Strange. I never noticed that street before. I could have sworn I knew every street in the neighborhood.

Dirk's musings were interrupted by a loud thud. In his entryway lay a bulky package, "DIRK QUIGBY" emblazoned in fiery letters.

Dirk hauled it into the living room and tore it open. Inside was a large manuscript, bound in dark wine-red leather. It was warm to the touch and read, "World Religion and Afterlife 101."

Amazing, how on earth could they possibly deliver so quickly? This is a first-class operation ... or they are desperate for enrollment.

He pulled out the manuscript and, beer in hand, began perusing the contents.

Dirk could not remember afterward what he had read, or indeed even if he *had* read. But that night he dreamed of burgundy manuscripts and warm vellum pages covered in arcane symbols. As he watched, the black letters changed to scuttling crabs racing along the pages. The vellum uncurled, turning into a sandy shore along an azure sea.

The Book of Job

Oh, you hate your job? There's a support group for that. It's called
EVERYBODY and they meet at the bar. —Drew Carey

Pesky, Pesky, & Pesky, Inc. had been founded in 1910 by Ivan Peskey-venovitch. Migrating to the sunny West, Pesky Senior had doffed his winter coat and the *-venovitch*, donned sunglasses, and gone into PR. In the old country he had sold potatoes; in the new one he would peddle dreams.

The company's mission was to come up with catchy jingles and slo-gans for its client's myriad products. But as with most companies, Pesky, Pesky, & Pesky, Inc. had been consumed by a mega-corporation. It now existed as one tentacle of a many-limbed conglomerate.

Dirk had tried to branch out into product creation; his ice-cream, "Goody Goody Gumdrops," was catchy, clever, and colorful. The only drawback was that gumdrops, when frozen, acquire the hardness of dia-monds. Luckily, the ice-cream was test-marketed in Mexico, where a few broken teeth were no big deal, easily bought off by a bag of beans and *manteca* or Corona beer. If "Goody Goody Gumdrops" had made it to the States, it would have been named "Class Action Crunch."

Pesky, Pesky, & Pesky, Inc. consisted of the copy writing team of Dirk Quigby, Matt Court, Angelica Far (who did voice-overs), and the Big Boss, Marcus Finkelstein. Angelica was Dirk's favorite. She was an attractive thirty-six, and the corners of her gray-green eyes creased with the remnants of laughter. Her thin, straight nose ended in a slope, which prevented it from being a classic. Her teeth were tiny and her mouth wide, exposing a generous amount of upper gum when she laughed, which was often. It might sound unappealing, but in Angelica, it was endearing.

Marcus Finkelstein had the charisma of a moist crumpet. He worshipped power and was both deceitful and boring, traits that might have conflicted in a crunchier individual. He was tall and almost bald, his domed head ringed by a fringe of brown frizz.

"He reminds me of a mutant cue ball," Dirk said.

"Don't be so hard on him," Angelica said, "The poor man is just dealing with the stress of being a dickhead. Remember, *stressed* spelled backwards is *dickhead*."

Dirk's office was situated in a soulless glass and chrome building, on the thirteenth floor, which tradition and superstition had renumbered. It was erroneously referred to as the fourteenth floor, but Dirk was not fooled. He knew that no matter the machinations of man, thirteen, not fourteen, followed twelve. Call it what they would, he worked on the thirteenth floor.

The office contained three colorless cubicles composed of pressed innards from an ancient forest. There was a small airless conference room for meetings and a huge airy corner office for Marcus.

Dirk sat in his cube, gazing blankly at the project before him. *How to make laxative sexy?* Picture a hunk lifting weights; an incredibly sexy girl enters; full lips pout, "He's known for his smooth moves. Shouldn't you be? Buy Bowel Pal."

"'Bowel Pal, huh?'" Angelica said, leaning over his shoulder. "Great product name. Do you remember about fifteen or twenty years ago there was a diet candy called 'Ayds'? It was supposed to help you lose weight."

"Yeah," Dirk chuckled, "One of the best product names of all time. How about 'Black Death Bonbons'?"

"Or Gonorrhea Gummy Bears?"

"Herpes Hard Suckers."

"Plague Pralines."

"Chlamydia Candy."

A shadow fell across Dirk's desk.

"So what's going on here?" Marcus asked.

"Oh, just thinking outside the box, putting our heads together. There is no 'I' in *team*, you know," Angelica said, walking back toward her desk.

Marcus narrowed his eyes, "So, how's the Bowel Pal copy coming?"

"Great," Dirk sighed, turning toward his computer screen and willing Marcus to vanish.

"You need to challenge yourself, Dirk, okaaay? You have a tendency to go for the low-hanging fruit. You need to make them want to buy! You need to infuse it into their drinking water!"

Dirk nodded, and Marcus turned back to his office.

Of course I go for the low-hanging fruit, thought Dirk in irritation. *It's there, it's ripe. First I gather it, then I go for the high stuff. Why let the low-hanging fruit rot? I'd like to infuse something into his damn drinking water.*

For the rest of the day Dirk sat in his cell, feeling the precious minutes of his life tick by. He was thinking outside the box, all right—thinking how to escape his box and the whole damn building, never to return. Thinking that his life, any life, must have a greater purpose than making laxative alluring.

Once, Dirk had posted funny or inspiring quotes on the porous walls of his compartment. Over the years these had slowly been replaced by award-winning ads, lists of contacts, and snappy slogans. The only reminder from a time when Dirk had attempted to personalize his beige box was a small faded photo of his sister, Mary, tucked in a corner.

Neither Dirk's mother nor grandmother had been particularly maternal. They lavished their affections on objects other than their progeny. Lulu was designed by nature to be a party girl; she thoroughly resented the intrusion of children into her life. Lacking education and despising introspection, she largely left Dirk to his own devices, and Mary to Dirk.

Mary had been two years younger than him. They had grown up together, allies against the pressures of trying to fit in a world that applauded jocks and cheerleaders. When only twenty-four, Mary had been killed in a freak accident. Dirk missed her.

★

Dirk was jolted out of his reverie by the braying of Marcus, making his post-meeting rounds. Dirk eyed his approach warily. *So, what's it going to be this time,* he wondered glumly.

"Great News, Buddy! You, Dirk Quigby, are being promoted! You are now the director of our travel division!"

"I didn't know we had a travel division."

"We don't, or rather we didn't ... but, now we DO! Okaaay? And you, Dirk Quigby, are going to head it! 'Special Travel Destinations.'"

STDs, Dirk thought. *It could be worse.*

Thus began Dirk's new job, journeying toward his dreams. He would be traveling to exotic places, and though not exactly writing the great American novel, at least writing. He could take notes and one day ...

But there were three problems. First, Dirk was not allowed out of his cube. His job, after all, was not to travel, but to sell. Instead of becoming a journeying journeyman, he spent his days watching reel after reel of horrendous film clips and pouring over illiterate brochures. Secondly, the "Special" destinations were not places Dirk or anyone else would be eager to visit. Thirdly, instead of producing deathless prose, or even entertaining editorials, Dirk was writing billboard slogans. What could be more innovative than plastering travel destinations on the road? Besides, one arm of Pesky, Pesky & Pesky, Inc. owned an embarrassment of billboards.

It wasn't worse than writing mottos for laxatives, but that was only because writing mottos for laxatives was shit.

11

STDs ... Shitty travel destinations, Dirk thought darkly. *Places to make you appreciate home.*

"Watts—it's a riot!"

"Tora Bora. Cavern tours daily."

"Sierra Leone ... You think you've got it bad?"

To make it all worse, Angelica was out sick, home with a head cold. Dirk looked at his picture of Mary and sighed.

And So It Came To Pass

Peculiar travel suggestions are dancing lessons from God.
—Kurt Vonnegut

Once home, Dirk showered, changing into jeans and his favorite sweatshirt. He got back in his car driving toward Elysium College. To his surprise, the street he'd never noticed was just where the map said it would be.

Elysium lay at the end of a cul-de-sac. It was a low stucco building, a classic example of fast-profit/flat-box architecture. Dirk entered, and saw the Cary Grant stand-in he had seen the night before.

What a Mickey Mouse operation. They can't even afford to hire actors!

The room, a windowless rectangle, was filled with rows of tiny wooden desks attached to tiny cramped seats. At the front of the room, the dark, handsome instructor leaned nonchalantly against a sarcophagus of a desk, one leg carelessly draped over the edge.

"Come in, come in," the stranger said with forced jollity. His dark eyes were ringed by dark circles. In person, he was noticeably weary. "I am here to answer all your questions."

I doubt that.

The room brought back memories. How much of his childhood, youth, and young manhood had been wasted in rooms like this? The blackboard clouded gray with the dust of fruitless equations; the smell of chalk filled Dirk's nostrils.

"I know, you doubt that. I realize that you feel your questions about the afterlife cannot be easily answered."

They can't be answered at all; the only way to answer them would be to visit different afterlives.

"I know," the stranger said tiredly, "The only way is to visit each afterlife."

"What?" Dirk squeaked, alarmed into full attention for the first time in years. *I didn't say anything!*

"Well," the stranger continued, swinging his leg back and forth against the desk, "I rather just assumed that like any normal person, you feel the need for personal experience. Your life, your work, has made you cynical. Not in a bad way," the stranger hastily amended, "in a good, a very good, completely clear-headed, totally rational way. Who among us doesn't want firsthand knowledge?"

True, Dirk thought grudgingly. He sat on one of the tiny desks. It was not comfortable. "Hey," Dirk questioned, "how do you know what I do?"

"The form you filled out on the Internet."

"Oh," Dirk felt reassured. Even though he did not remember filling out a form.

"As part of our first-time offer only," the stranger continued with a pretense of enthusiasm, "we are prepared to offer you exactly what you want: a firsthand visit, not just to one, but to multiple Heavens."

"Right," Dirk said. So, who are you—God?"

"Do I look like God?" the stranger asked wearily.

Dirk shook his head.

"Okay, no more beating around the bush then. Let me introduce myself. Lucifer, at your service." He mocked a courtly bow.

Although Dirk had managed to ignore his television's color and the amazingly rapid book delivery, now it all came flooding back to him. Tensing, he upset the desk and crashed to the floor. The desk tottered back and forth like a decapitated rocking horse before collapsing onto Dirk's legs.

Lucifer extended a beautiful hand.

"B-b-but," Dirk stammered from his seat on the floor, unconscious of the desk trapping his legs, "even if I believed you, which I most certainly do not, what would be the point of trading my soul for a premature glimpse of Heaven? It'd be like spending all your money to find the perfect house, then not being able to buy it because you were out of cash." Dirk knew that this was just some sort of a ridiculous publicity stunt; nonetheless, he was breathing hard and fast.

"I assure you, my friend, the very last thing I want is your soul. Do you know how overcrowded Hell is?"

Cary—or Lucifer—haggardly raked a hand though his glossy, dark curls. Dirk noticed he was graying at the temples.

"I thought it would be a lot more enjoyable," Lucifer explained. "At first it was, Hell contained only a few thousand souls. I had enough time and room that I could sort of tailor Hell to their needs.

"Now, most people don't even try to get into Heaven, and if they do, they often go about it in very disturbing ways. I don't care what you've heard; blowing up people is not the way into Heaven. Neither is blowing up medical clinics. In fact, I think it'd be safe to say that usually bombs, guns, and killing don't make for easy access. Then, there are all those folks who are eligible, but make it so damned hard on themselves! The Catholics all have to go to Purgatory first, and who do you think has to arrange for that?"

"Then there are the Jehovah's Witnesses. When they get up to Heaven, what do they do? They start counting, for Christ's sake! They believe Heaven only has room for 144,000 souls. Of course all the slots are full, and who do you think gets stuck with the overflow?"

He gestured in irritated fatigue at himself.

"Then there's the idea of Hell. What with overpopulation and global warming, Hell compares very favorably to New York or Tokyo on a hot day. Take the burning flames; I mean, how much pain can you feel when you're dead? One of the things about being dead is that you aren't very sensitive! Anyway," Lucifer sighed, "I don't mean to complain, but if I'd have known what it was going to be like, I'd have much, much rather served in Heaven.

"So, as you can see, my offer is entirely without strings. Your soul is and will remain your own—I don't want it," he added emphatically. "Whatdaya say? Would you, Dirk Quigby, like to be the first person ever on the face of this planet to traverse the afterlife and live to tell the tale?" The Devil forced an insincere grin and extended his hand, "Shall we shake on it?"

"Okay," Dirk said, pushing the desk off his legs but remaining on the floor. "But even if I play along, what's in it for you? I mean, if you're the Devil, you can't be doing this out of the goodness of your heart, right? Hell, you probably don't even have a heart."

"Well," the Devil replied cautiously, "I do want something in return, sort of a quid pro quo."

"Ah ha!" Dirk smirked.

"It's not a bad deal," the Devil pleaded, "just hear me out."

Dirk folded his arms and gave Lucifer a dubious stare.

Lucifer sighed. "Look, it's hell being me. I mean it. I thought it would be entertaining, and in the beginning it had its rewards. Either I'd acquire exceptional souls like Galileo or Leonardo, who weren't evil but weren't allowed into the Heaven of their age, or I'd get vicious scum like Hitler or Genghis Khan, who were rather amusing to torment. But now, it's every Tom, Dick, and Mohammed! Some of them are pretty snotty, too. They keep asking, 'Where are the virgins? Where are the virgins!?' I tell them, 'Look, it's Hell. No virgins in Hell, okay?' But, they just won't listen! Finally, I figured it out. I give them virgins now, but they never get to have intercourse with them. That way I can save the virgins for the next fanatic who comes down the pipeline. Of course the girls are about two thousand years old by now, so it's really not much of a temptation anyway."

"I still don't know what you want from me," Dirk said.

"Ahhhh, well, here's where you come in. I think if more people were sort of … encouraged to go to Heaven … You're an ad man. You know … make it sexy. Highlight the benefits and downplay the difficulty."

"So what exactly are you asking me to do?"

"Well," the Devil said, nervously tugging at a forelock, "I'd like you to write … you know … sort of a guide to the afterlife. Touch on the different kinds of Heavens …"

"Let me get this straight … you want me to write a Zagat Guide to the afterlife?"

"Well," Lucifer replied, "in a nutshell … yes."

Dirk was silent for a moment, a million diverse thoughts all scampering in different directions inside his head.

"I'm just curious … Why me? I mean, I know I can write. I'm good at snappy slogans—but come on, I'm no Hemingway."

"Do you know how much Hemingway would cost? Besides, he's dead. He's already chosen his afterlife."

"Where did he go?"

"That," Lucifer grinned, "is private. Your choice of afterlife is as sacrosanct as a pre-Watergate psychiatrist's office. Just look at the tabloids—there are oodles of Elvis sightings in Memphis or Lynchburg, but you never read about whether he's in the Baptist Heaven or the Buddhist one.

"As to why you … well, you have experience writing about unplea … unusual places."

Dirk was a tad nervous that the Devil might want him to sign a contract in blood, especially if it was to be his own blood. Lucifer just laughed.

"Oh no, that's only Hollywood. A handshake is as good as a promise." And so saying, the Devil once again extended his hand.

Dirk took it, feeling the smooth flesh that generated a curious warmth. It was what a satin electric blanket might have felt like. Dirk noticed Lucifer's graying temples were now coal black.

"Good as a promise," Lucifer repeated, enclosing Dirk's hand in a firm yet delicate grip.

Looking deep into Lucifer's lustrous black eyes, Dirk thought he saw the faintest suggestion of a spark, a tiny flame that contained within it a guarantee—that a promise to Satan was good as an oath, and an oath to the Devil was not to be taken lightly.

Dirk felt a brief but burning stab in his eyes.

"Ow," he cried, instinctively pulling away from Lucifer, "What was that?"

"Nothing to worry about," Lucifer assured him. "It's The Devil's press pass. I sear it onto your retinas so that you never have to worry about losing it."

That is not foremost in my current list of concerns.

Lucifer turned to leave.

"But how will I get there?" Dirk cried out.

"Oh, don't worry about that," Lucifer replied, "The afterlife is always much closer than people think."

The Book of the Dead

A baby is God's opinion that life should go on. —Carl Sandburg

Dirk was nervous. He sat in his apartment waiting. He was not sure how or when he would depart. About that, Lucifer, that Devil, had been maddeningly vague. He walked to the refrigerator, took out a beer, and returned to the overstuffed couch. Dirk slumped down into billowy pillows. He pulled out a cigarette, thumbed his lighter and inhaled deeply.

Was there really life after death?

Grasping the beer between his thighs, Dirk popped the top.

With a *Whoosh!* he was thrown backward. He felt his body being wrung into a narrow and sinuous shape, kind of like a liquid towel. It was not a pleasant sensation. As his body elongated and swirled into a funnel, Dirk saw his reflection whirling back at him from a window.

YIKESsss …

This was his last semi-cogent thought before he was whirled, swirled, and sucked down the beer bottle.

He awoke, sopping, shivering, and dripping beer, feet firmly planted on earth. Before him loomed an enormous pyramid, with an archway leading into darkness. Gazing into the hole, Dirk got a sick feeling in his stomach. He did not like dark, dank places in the earth.

This is heaven? He straightened his shoulders and headed down, down, down into the afterlife of ancient Egypt.

DIRK QUIGBY'S GUIDE TO THE ANCIENT EGYPTIAN AFTERLIFE

Note: This is currently a "closed Heaven"—closed because this religion is no longer practiced. However it is still possible to gain entry. All you *need is someone to mummify you and a personalized copy of the Book of the Dead.*

END DESTINATION:

All those who pass the tests of the underworld may enter the Blessed Land, which is a lot like the land of the living, except that it lacks sorrow, pain, and is underground.

In this afterlife, you are the proud possessor of three souls.

The Ka, created at conception, is an exact replica of you. The Ka is trapped within your heart and expelled by death. It has to stay close to you and can never leave the tomb. The Ka will die unless your body remains inviolate. If your body is not correctly mummified, the Ka can live inside a picture of the body on the wall of the tomb, *but it's not much of a life.* The Ka requires daily deliveries of fresh food and drink. *It is particularly fond of frappuccinos.*

The second soul is the Ba, *referred to by apostates as the Ba-humbug.* It represents your individuality. The Ba lives in the tomb but can come and go as it pleases. When visiting the land of the living, it can take on any form it wants to.

The third is the immortal Akh, which journeys through the underworld.

In order for these spirits to survive, your body has to be properly preserved. As this is an extremely costly procedure, usually only pharaohs make it to the afterlife.

When you die, your body is taken to the embalmer. A cut is made in the left side of your abdomen. Since it is a stoneable offense to harm the body of the pharaoh, even after death, the person who makes the cut is chased away and has rocks thrown at him. *This job has very high turnover, lousy benefits, and no dental.*

The brain is useless; the heart does all thinking. Therefore, all the organs except the brain must be preserved. The brain is pulled out through the nose and discarded. *The deceased pharaoh who I questioned agreed that the brain is useless, then immediately forgot the question.*

All organs are removed and stored in canopic jars. The body is packed with salt. For forty days and forty nights, it salts.

Then the body is wrapped in bandages layered with jewelry and amulets. The tomb is filled with furniture, food, carved statues, and games designed to make the afterlife more fun.

The last ritual is the "Opening of the Mouth." This ceremony restores full use of all bodily functions. The Opening of the Mouth can also endow statues with the ability to eat, breathe, see, and hear, *and play cribbage with your Ka. The Ka's I met appeared almost obsessed with cribbage. The championships were even more vicious than those I remember from college!*

If you want, you can mummify your favorite pet to take with you. *Don't forget the pet treats.*

After you are mummified, you are carried in state to your tomb. At the end of the funeral procession stagger professional mourners, women dressed in blue, who wail, scream, and tear their hair. *Rainy days and mummies really get me down.*

The journey into the afterlife is difficult.

You begin your journey by crossing a wide river, which is guarded by monsters. The trip culminates in the "Hall of Two Truths." Here you must answer accusations concerning forty-two crimes. *Unfortunately, this is not multiple-choice, although it is open-book of the dead.* As you counter these charges, your heart is put on a scale and weighed against a feather, which represents truth. If your heart is lighter than the feather, you can join the gods. If it is heavier, a monster that is part crocodile, part lion, and part hippopotamus will consume your body. After the heart is consumed, you will cease to exist.

Usually, only the pharaohs were lucky enough to get to the feather test, and even though I'm certain that many of them were fine gentlemen, this Heaven was almost empty. In fact, there was only one pharaoh in evidence. He was an infant.

If accepted into the afterlife, you will be asked by Osiris to perform some menial, agricultural task *such as deadheading his flower garden or weed-whacking his lawn.*

Statues, "shabtis," will have been left inside your tomb. These statues are reputed to come to life and will do the gardening for you. *I asked the infant pharaoh about this, but he only gazed at me blankly, reiterated the uselessness of the brain, shook his sacred rattle, and wet himself.*

ENTRY REQUIREMENTS:

Each region of Egypt had its own special god. There was Thoth, the god of sacred writings and wisdom, who looked like a baboon; Sekhmet, the mistress of war and sickness, *who was never invited to parties,* and about two thousand others.

The first God was Re (Ra), the sun god. Re was the creator of life, the universe, and everything. He was also Osiris' dad.

Osiris had many titles: King of the Dead, God of Agriculture, *CEO of* the underworld, Fertility, Controller of Nile floods, and *Assistant* Manager of the rising and setting of the sun.

His brother Set lured him into a coffin, *telling him it was a new type of greenhouse,* and sent him down the Nile. The coffin washed ashore in Lebanon, where a tree encased it. The king of Lebanon was bowled over by the grandeur, girth, and beauty of the tree, so he chopped it down.

Meanwhile, back in Egypt ... Isis, protective goddess of women, learned of Osiris' death. Isis was doubly fond of Osiris, being both his sister and wife.

She found Osiris' body and intended to resurrect him, but Set stole the pieces, scattering them throughout Egypt. Isis collected the pieces and breathed life into them.

Osiris rose, a god-king; "but nothing that has died, not even a god, may dwell in the land of the living." He was forced into retirement, *given a gold watch,* and became King of the Underworld. He had one final night on Earth, and what a night it was! He impregnated his sister/savior Isis, who conceived Horus, *acclaimed for hatching a Who.*

Horus (aka Haroeris, Harpocrates, Harsiesis, Re-Harakhty) became sky-god and living king. To avenge his dad, he fought Set. Horus carelessly lost an eye, which keeps reappearing all over, on amulets, dollar bills, and Masonic temples. Finally Horus defeated Set and castrated him … *from which we derive the expression "an eyeball for a ball."* Set was cast into darkness, where he remains sore and ornery to this day. In the last days, Horus and Set will fight again. Set will be defeated, and Osiris will return. On that day, the Day of Awakening, all the tombs shall open, the just dead shall live, and sorrow shall pass away.

The spells and rituals cast by Isis, and others, were collected into the *Book of Going Forth by Day*, usually known as the *Book of the Dead*. This book, personalized for each dead person, contains about two hundred magical spells, sexual texts, songs, and pictures, which help in navigating the afterlife. Karma Sutra for Corpses.

QUALITY RATINGS (ONE- TO FIVE-STAR):
Perks: ★★ —You CAN take it with you.
Food: ★★ —Bread is the main dish here, sometimes supplemented

by fricasseed ox in a fig reduction sauce. It is always accompanied by barley beer.

Drink: ★★ —Barley beer is like the sun god: it burns going down, but afterward I felt immortal!

Music: ★ —I've never been partial to the blues.

Accommodations: ★★ —Very spacious, but dark. If you enjoy solitude and spelunking, this just might be the afterlife for you.

Entry Requirements: ★ —(The more stars the easier the entry.)

OVERALL RATING: ★★

Plop.

Dirk found himself on his sofa once more. He looked at the clock mounted on his wall; the time read 6:15 PM. How could that be? He had departed at 6 PM on Saturday; surely he'd been gone more than fifteen minutes. Glancing down at his wristwatch, he discovered it read 8 PM, but instead of the date reading 2/16, as it had done when he had left, it now read 2/18. According to his watch, he had been gone for two days. Dirk ran a hand through his hair. How was this possible? He turned on his computer; it read 2/16. Checking the dates on his answering machine and microwave produced the same results: the mechanical chroniclers agreed it was 2/16. Had he really been gone for only fifteen minutes? It sure seemed more like two days.

Dirk wanted a drink, but he feared that beer might have become his portal into another dimension. As he did not desire another immediate trip to Heaven, he refrained. A few minutes, or two days, later, depending on your point of reference, a dirty Dirk rose from his couch and strode toward his shower.

If it didn't require so much prep, it wouldn't be so bad. I'd miss the light, but I've seen worse. Hell, I've written copy for worse. It's the Ba who has it best—gets to go wherever it wants and changes shape at will. Yep, no doubt about it, I wanna be my Ba.

He had a cigarette, brushed his teeth, and went to bed.

Dirk still spent his days in captivity at Pesky, Pesky & Pesky, Inc., but now instead of merely being bored and frustrated, he was tense—very tense. For all he knew, at any moment he might be whirled into an afterlife. He had no time to shape his notes into any kind of workable document and he had no way to contact Lucifer. Although Dirk was relieved that death did not equal annihilation, the Egyptian afterlife was not reassuring; it didn't make any more sense to Dirk than life. Dirk had not had a revelation. He did not have a greater comprehension of the universe. He was not illuminated. Heaven appeared as petty and as bounded by hollow rituals and empty rules as Earth. Now, however, he had two jobs instead of one.

At last Dirk was a traveler. But not a happy one.

Inside the Box

*When did I realize I was God? Well, I was praying
and I suddenly realized I was talking to myself.*
—Peter Barnes

Dirk did not like work. He did not enjoy manufacturing mendacious mottos. Most of all, he loathed the mandatory weekly meetings.

Marcus began each with an exercise in team building.

"Today we are going to take the bull by the horns! Okaaay?" Marcus triumphantly reached into a bag at his feet and pulled out a thoroughly sterilized pair of antlers. (It was a big bag.)

Marcus thrust the antlers at Dirk. "How's that feel?" Marcus crowed, punching Dirk vigorously on the biceps.

"Like dead deer antlers."

Marcus's eyes narrowed and his lips pursed. "Well, for now they're bull horns—okaaay. It was the closest thing I could find. You're copy writers; you must have an imagination—so use it! Okaaay? Think outside the box! So what are these?"

"Bull horns," Dirk replied.

"Let me hear you say, 'I'm gonna take the bull by the horns this week!' Say it loud, say it proud!"

"I'm going to take the bull by the horns this week," Dirk repeated glumly.

The horns were passed around the table, each copy writer grabbing them so all could feel bull hemoglobin coursing through their veins and into their sales potential.

Dirk slunk into his cubical. Today's mission: Downtown Oakland.

At 5 PM Friday, Dirk turned off his computer and went home. He was a nervous wreck. When awake, he was worried about how or when he would be whisked to his next afterlife. When he slept, he was haunted by visions of Oakland, with its decided dearth of Oaks.

Greek to Me

We climb mountains because they are there, and worship
God because He is not. —Mignon McLaughlin

Dirk was awaked by the alarm, not a pleasant sound. Staggering out of bed he reeled to the microwave to heat up water for coffee.

Instant was fine. Dirk could never understand people who made a religion out of coffee. Grinding beans, steaming milk … the last thing Dirk desired in the morning was a ritual, at least not before coffee. The point of coffee was to be brown, warm, and full of caffeine. Taste buds are late sleepers.

Discovering he was out of milk, Dirk cursed softly. But after a cup of instant espresso, he was ready, if not to face the day, at least drive to the corner for some milk. Dirk got into his car and turned the key. The air conditioner instantly whirled to life. This was odd, because Dirk didn't have an air conditioner. Before he could begin to wonder, he felt an odd yet familiar twisting sensation. Although his hands clutched helplessly at the steering wheel, he was relentlessly pulled toward the vents.

This sucks, he thought as he whirled into darkness.

He awoke, windblown and tousled, in a clean golden city in the clouds.

DIRK QUIGBY'S GUIDE TO THE ANCIENT GREEK AFTERLIFE

Note: This was my second "closed Heaven." Due to the often-conflicting beliefs among the denizens of this Paradise, Mount Olympus has been subdivided into various neighborhoods separated by an opaque mist. The inhabitants appear blissfully unaware of the confines of their reality.

END DESTINATION:

Mount Olympus. Great mountain views. Fine dining, plush couches, beautiful boys.

If you have not made enough accepted sacrifices, you will end up in Hades. There, Hades reigns over drifting crowds of shadowy figures—"shades" of all who have died. It's not the best place to spend eternity, but for Hades, it's not so bad. As for Olympus ...

ENTRY REQUIREMENTS:

You need to worship twelve major deities and a host of minor ones, but if you manage to please even one of the Big Twelve, you'll be in like Flynn.

Make sacrifices to said deities. Accepted sacrifices usually consist of sheep, cows, goats, pigs, bulls, and the occasional human. The really sweet part of this, generally speaking, is that you need to offer your chosen deity only the blood, bones, and hide of the victim. You get to eat the rest.

Be buried with your possessions so you can carry them with you into the next life.

If fortunate enough to possess wives and slaves, kill and bury them nearby, so you won't be lonely on the Mount.

QUALITY RATINGS:

Perks: ★ ★ ★ ★ —Great views; alpine air; teeming with beautiful fruit-serving boys.

Music: ★ ★ ★ —Varies from simple homey (or Homeric) lute pieces to rather grand orchestral numbers.

Food: ★ ★ ★ —You name it, it's here, except for the New World veggies (tomatoes, corn, potatoes, and avocados, etc.). On the downside there is no chocolate and a dearth of pasta. If you can't die without Italian food, go elsewhere.

Drink: ★ ★ ★ ★ —Is enjoyed while reclining on couches and pillows. There is a wonderful selection of wine for every palate.

Accommodations: ★ ★ ★ ★ —Luxurious.

Entry Requirements: ★ ★ ★ ★ (Unless you are a wife or slave, which is generally difficult everywhere.)

OVERALL RATING: ★ ★ ★ ★ (Except for wives and slaves as noted above.)

Although he had departed via air conditioner, Dirk returned to his couch five minutes or twenty-four hours later.

Weird, maybe electronics don't work in Heaven. Maybe watches require substantial reality to run?

The Greek afterlife was fabulous. I'm not into young boys, but if you want women, they let you have women … As long as you aren't a woman, everything's great. The requirements aren't too arduous, either.

Too bad the Mount's closed; it's really a lovely development.

Dirk had a beer and went to bed to grab a few hours of sleep.

Angelic Voices

More tears are shed over answered prayers, than unanswered ones.
—Teresa of Avila

Dirk arrived at Pesky, Pesky & Pesky, Inc. at 10:30, rather the worse for wear. He was unshaven, with odors of stale beer, cigarettes, and a wild variety of heavenly incense clinging to him. Marcus Finkelstein eyed him disapprovingly.

"Good of you to join us," Marcus said.

Dirk slunk into his cube. He'd rather hoped to slither under the radar today, and maybe hack some order into his notes on original sin.

"So how's the new director of STDs?" breathed a honeyed voice.

Dirk was caught off guard. What a voice! It was the kind of voice that could enter a man's dreams and make his nights rapturous, sensual delights. It was a voice that made his inside soft and his outside hard. Dirk turned.

"Angelica?!"

"I still have a cold," she explained, "Frog in my throat."

"That's a hell of a foxy frog," Dirk croaked.

The remainder of the morning passed quickly.

First, Dirk spent a few hours trying to come up with slogans to make Pyongyang, North Korea, an appealing travel destination. After a meandering Internet search, Dirk discovered that Pyongyang, in addition to having a brutal dictatorship, a history of human rights abuses, and yearly famines, also had a really nasty climate, ranging from brutal cold winds to sweltering heat and humidity, and back again to brutal cold winds.

Dirk clicked on some language site that was teaching useful phrases, such as "You are like a frog in a well."

He tried another language and history site and found:

"Han Guk … The word Gook (or Guk) means people … Han Gook is for Koreans and Mi Gook means Americans. During the Korean War the American soldiers were greeted with joy. After all, they were strong. They were tall. They were handsome. They carried big guns. Cries of 'Mi Gook, Mi Gook,' sounded across the sand.

"The soldiers, due to their intensive preparation in language, mores, and culture figured that the Koreans were saying 'Me Gook.' So they called them gooks. It was not until the Vietnam War that gook became a pejorative … useful for insulting any Asian."

Interesting, thought Dirk … although I'm not sure how to spin it.

Having run dry on ideas to make Pyongyang attractive, Dirk decided to finish an overdue ad for insect killer: "100% natural. 100% pure. Chemical-free. Kills bugs dead!"

"Well, you can't kill them alive," Angelica said, perching casually on the arm of his chair. Her voice, filled with sex, heat, and lust, unnerved him.

"Yeah," he replied hoarsely, "maybe I should say, 'sends bugs to bug heaven,' or, 'returns bugs to a new incarnation.'"

Angelica eyed him speculatively.

God! This double life is getting to me. Get a grip, boy. Get a grip!

"Well," said Dirk weakly, "I was just trying to make it more … uh—hey, it's lunch time! Would you care to join me?"

"After all this talk about pure poison and reincarnated bugs, how can I resist?"

"Yeah, who knows? Maybe our waiter will be a reincarnated cockroach."

"Hmmmm," said Angelica said, "Would that mean he'd been a good cockroach or a bad one?"

Coffee, Tea or ...?

Men are those creatures with two legs and eight hands.
—Jayne Mansfield

Under the thrall of Angelica's velvet voice, Dirk took her to lunch at a pricy nouveau cuisine restaurant that had opened recently. It was mod, it was new, it was hip ... the décor managed to be both incredibly ugly and hideously uncomfortable. The interior was so dark they had to squint their eyes into tiny slits and hold the menu very close to their faces—not attractive. On the other hand, it was dark, so neither could see the other's squashed visage.

The menu was incomprehensible to all but people with PhDs in arcane dialects, and the waiters exuded a superior air, content in the knowledge that only they had the intellectual capacity for understanding, much less pronouncing, the varied menu items. The dishes, which were listed in order of "esoteric vibrations," were all "infused" with "reductions."

A slim, blond young man escorted Angelica and Dirk to a booth in the back. "I'm Greg," he intoned snottily, "I'll be your waiter throughout the entire meal."

"Oh," Angelica whispered throatily, "I'm so glad that we aren't going to have to change waiters between courses."

Dirk was both amused and apprehensive. He had managed to glimpse the only comprehensible section of the menu, the price list. He fervently hoped Angelica's reference to "courses" had only been a joke.

His hopes were dashed, however, when Angelica began the meal with a cocktail and hors d'oeuvres, followed by soup, salad, pasta, fish, vegetables, and dessert, each accompanied by the appropriate wine, and finished off with ten-year-old port and an espresso. Dirk watched in amazed horror as slim Angelica ate and drank her way through enough food and drink to fill up Orson Welles (when he was alive). She appeared unaffected.

Dirk, assuring her that he was not hungry, rather glumly munched a wilted salad topped with an infusion of Caesar dressing and sun dried croutons.

"The food's not very good here," he commented, "But at least they give small portions. Why do you suppose that the octopus rates lower on esoteric vibration than scampi?"

Angelica considered this while chewing her cherry-almond-crusted trout, infused with a citrus-chili–chocolate sauce reduction. She delicately dabbed her lips with a teal napkin. "Perhaps it's because octopus have some rather unsavory sexual habits. Although amazingly smart and emotional, they can be quite savage, you know. When a male gets sexually excited, he becomes striped and horny … literally horny: two fleshy knobs just rise right out of his head.

"He doesn't have a penis, poor dear, but that doesn't stop him! One of his eight arms is hollow and he starts caressing the female all over— sometimes a tad violently. Then, he thrusts his hollow arm into the female's breathing cavity, and his sperm packets slide down his arm into her throat. If she doesn't like it, she may bite his arm off and swim around with it for days, until it absorbs into her body.

"In some species, the copulatory arm loads itself up with sperm, detaches itself from the octopus, and swims off by itself in search of a mate. Can you imagine how the female must feel? There she is, trying to nap perhaps, when suddenly she awakens to find a strange arm trying to force its way down her breathing passage and father her children."

"How on earth do you know that?" Dirk asked.

"Earth," she smiled, "has very little to do with it."

"Ah, yes. Well, how in oceans do you know then?"

"Oh, just interested I suppose. Earth really is a very diverse and lovely planet."

"Yes, it is," Dirk agreed wryly. "It's a good thing we work so hard to enhance it … making the world a better place, one ad at a time."

Angelica laughed a low, throaty sound that reached deep into Dirk's being and vibrated there, making him glad that he couldn't betray his feelings by the sudden protrusion of fleshy knobs rising from the top of his head.

★

Dirk spent the remainder of the day wracked in equal measure by pangs of hunger and horniness. The smooth chocolate richness of Angelica's new voice reverberated in his hollow soul, while the scant lettuce remnants of Caesar salad banged about his empty stomach.

That night he dreamed of floating in honeyed seas, pursued by a giant vagina that spurted croutons violently and ceaselessly in his direction.

Flat Earth Theory

In the beginning, there was nothing and God said "Let there be light," and there was still nothing but everybody could see it. —Dave Thomas

Ignoring both the two-week-wait rule as well as her obviously expensive eating habits, Dirk called Angelica the very next day and asked her to dinner. To his delight, she said yes.

Returning home from work, he showered and dried his hair. He examined himself in the mirror more closely and with more affection then he had for years. Tossing his hair back from his forehead, he smiled rakishly. Waggling a toothpick between his lips, he grabbed a Q-Tip and began to clean his ears.

At first he enjoyed the circular sensation, but the Q-Tip circled deeper and deeper. Dirk tried to pull it out of his ear but discovered, to his panic, that he had no control. With impossible, sickening determination, the Q-Tip burrowed deep inside Dirk's head, pulling a horrified, reversible Dirk into hidden darkness.

He awoke on a hot, flat, sunny plain. He had reached the Zoroastrian Heaven. Rising shakily to his feet, he wandered dazedly toward the waiting afterlife.

DIRK QUIGBY'S GUIDE
TO THE ZOROASTRIAN AFTERLIFE

Notes: Zoroastrianism goes back a long, long way. It is based on the revelations of the prophet Zarathushtra, who preached between the seventeenth and fifteenth centuries BC in Iran. "Zarathushtra" means "possessor of golden camels." Sadly, I did not see any of these marvelous

beasts. *Providentially for Zarathushtra, he was assassinated at seventy-seven. Martyrdom is an almost foolproof way to ensure that your teachings will be taken seriously, and seventy-seven is a damn fine age at which to be martyred.* Zarathushtra preached a moral dualism between Ahura Mazda (no relation to the car), the Lord of Wisdom, and Angra Mainyu, the Devil.

Because a perfect being cannot create that which is not perfect, Zoroastrians believe that all evil, darkness, cold, ill health, pain, suffering, and death, taxes, and visits from one's mother-in-law are caused by Angra Mainyu.

END DESTINATION:

A flat, warm, day-lit Earth.

ENTRY REQUIREMENTS:

Ahura Mazda created six spiritual beings: Ameretat (plants), Haurvata (water), Spenta Armaiti (earth), Asha Vahishta (fire), Khshathra Vairya (metal), and Vohu Manah (wisdom, represented by an ox). *Although I do not have a close personal relationship with many oxen, the ones I know are not noted for their cognitive abilities.* There are also some lesser spirits, like Anahita, the spirit of female fertility, *which I'd rank over metal ... but to each his own.*

When Ahura Mazda created the Earth, everything was perfect for six thousand years. Then the Devil entered, screwing it all up, creating evil, death, and a lot of other headaches, including headaches.

The current mixture of good and evil will last another six thousand years. It is our job as humans to root for Ahura Mazda. We can do this best by good thoughts, good words, and good deeds. If we act in concert with the aforementioned divine beings, we can defeat the Devil.

Bad news for you want-to-be Zoroastrians: you must be born a

Zoroastrian; no converts welcome.

Death requires lots of preparation. In your final hours, recite a prayer of repentance and drink haoma, a kind of ephedra. *Not only do you get to go to heaven, you'll be thin! If there is no haoma around you can imbibe really old Gatorade. If this does not make you want to die, nothing will.*

Face south, the direction of Heaven and warmth.

Three is a very holy number. Utilize it whenever practical.

Burial takes place during the day, because cold and night are evil and of the Devil. Not a good time to meet your maker.

Death is bad, very, very bad. It is also unnatural and evil. In fact, you just can't say enough rotten things about death. Therefore, a dead body should not be buried, cremated, or set out to sea because it pollutes the earth, fire, or water. The corpus should be put in a tower facing the purity of the rising sun and left to be torn apart by vultures, *who have strong constitutions and can handle it.*

Each human has five parts: a body that unites with earth, a life force that joins the winds, a mortal soul that becomes immortal, and a prototype that teams up with the soul. After death, demons and good spirits vie for the soul. Evil is kept at bay by fire and light. After four days of this struggle, the good soul smells fragrant perfume and the bad soul smells noxious odors. *I didn't know that souls had noses!*

Three beneficent spirits guide good souls to the bridge of the Accumulator, *an ancestor of Arnold Schwarzenegger.* A tribunal gathers on the bridge to judge the soul. *Why this is necessary, as the good souls have already been separated from the bad by smells and spirits, I don't know.* If the soul belongs to a bad Zoroastrian or an unbeliever, three demons fetter it and drag it to the bridge. *I found this a tad harsh as, if you are not born a Zoroastrian, you are doomed to be a nonbeliever.*

This bridge connects the material realm to the spiritual one. It starts in the North, near Hell *and Texas*, and ends in the South, near Heaven.

Hell, where bad souls will dwell till the end of time, lies below the bridge. Hell is exceedingly nasty, filled with darkness and scorpions. It has a few descending levels: bad thought, bad speech, bad action, and *completely bad.*

Good souls dwell in Heaven till the end of time. Heaven consists of four ascending levels. The levels are beautiful gardens where you hang out with God, the other divinities, and all virtuous dead souls.

Confused souls hang out in Limbo till—you guessed it—the end of time. This however, is not as final as it sounds. The end of time is not eternity, after all: eternity can't end.

QUALITY RATINGS:

Perks: ★★★ —Eventually all the souls from Heaven, Hell, and Limbo will be resurrected on Earth for the final judgment. Good souls will rejoice, bad and limbo-ish souls will repent, everyone will go to Heaven, *and everyone gets a car!* The Devil will be sealed in molten metal. Human history will end. Everyone will dwell in happiness on a refurbished flat earth warmed by sunlight, lacking cold or night. *Everyone, that is, except for astronomers and winter sports enthusiasts.*

Music: ★ —I believe it's an acquired taste, best attained before the afterlife.

Food: ★★★ —Melons are quite popular here, and very good too. I also enjoyed nuts, dried fruit, vegetables, meat, rice potpourri, and fish stuffed with spice rolled in banana leaves.

Drink: ★★ —I had some rather too-sweet wines, also a clear liquid that burned like holy fire and made me feel heavenly.

Accommodations: ★★★ —Lovely gardens littered with luxurious couches.
Entry Requirements: ★★★
OVERALL RATING: ★★★

Plop! Dirk was back on his couch again. Looking at the clock, he realized that if he hurried, he wouldn't even be late to pick up Angelica.

Of Dachshunds and Diamonds

In the ultimate analysis, everything is incomprehensible.
—Thomas Henry Huxley

Due to the demands of his diminishing bank account, Dirk took Angelica to a cheap Mexican dive, where the food, although less esoteric, had the benefit of being copious and comprehensive. Both wines and sauces fit neatly under the appellations "white," "red," or "green."

Their waiter arrived.

"Are there any specials tonight?" Dirk asked.

"Special tonight … yes, it's 'red' tonight. You should've been here last night."

"Why? Was it 'green' last night?"

"No, last night it was red too. Green is tomorrow—better make a reservation now. We are filling up fast. Would you like red or white with your red?"

Both Angelica and Dirk decided to have red with their red.

After dinner, Dirk invited Angelica in for a nightcap. He was rather amazed that she could fit anything more into her svelte body, but she appeared insatiate.

They sat side by side on his overstuffed couch and sipped Merlot. Angelica munched some ancient Oreos Dirk had managed to scrounge up.

As the last Oreo vanished, Dirk, almost without volition, felt his lips drawn to hers. Five minutes later they were naked and she was sucking his toes.

As with most modern courtships, lunch followed dinner (and Oreos), and they proceeded into the bedroom as rapidly as night follows day.

★

Dirk lay in bed, lightly running his hand over the silhouette of Angelica's body. She smelled like a heady mixture of musk, lilacs, and freshly-mown grass.

"I wish," Angelica said, "this moment could go on forever—no more office, no more traffic, no more Marcus, no more writing deception, and no more jobs. I've had way too many rotten jobs."

He sighed, "Jobs are something I could probably live without."

"What would you do then? I mean if you could live without one."

Dirk considered this. "What I'd really like is to have 'fuck-you' money. Invent something simple and useful that reaps huge gobs of cash and sets me free. I don't want things, just time and freedom."

"Interesting, isn't it? We imagine that longing for money to buy time and freedom is somehow superior to lusting for money to buy stuff. So, do you have any ideas, like reinventing the paper clip?"

"Actually, I have tons of ideas. Wanna hear a recent one? I got the notion when they were wiring our office for the new plasma screen."

"Plasma," Angelica mused. "I know neon is produced by sending gas though glass tubes. Do you suppose that plasma is produced by filling tubes with human plasma?"

Dirk laughed. He looked almost handsome, with the disillusionment wiped briefly from his features. "It would make sense if plasma TVs are filled with plasma. Probably takes the blood of forty-seven street people to make one 32-inch plasma screen operable. But the clarity is astounding. A really cheap set is likely filled with Haitian baby plasma ... sure it's more than forty-seven of them ... but they're doomed anyway. Might as well not let them go to waste. Besides, I sent twenty-five dollars to the Katrina victims and gave some canned okra to the food bank, so why feel guilty?"

Angelica chuckled ruefully and ran her hand through his thick, glossy hair.

"Well that certainly explains the blood bank crisis," she said. "Also why Panasonic is investing in Urgent Care clinics."

"'Plasma' gives me the creeps," Dirk said, "'Plasma screen' sounds like it might just ooze out of its frame and engulf me by osmosis. That's what I feel the telly is trying to do." He shuddered. "Trying to engulf us, telling us we aren't good looking enough, thin enough, smart enough, beautiful enough, lucky enough, and rich, rich, rich enough ... that if we only have whiter teeth, breath like roses, a plasma TV, and join the Church of the one and only true God, we will have a perfect life and spend eternity in bliss.

"Still," he continued, "I have to admit the plasma TV is cool. It's large, has great color, and I've never seen better plasma!"

"Nothing better than good plasma," Angelica purred. "So, what was your brilliant, your plasma-inspired brainstorm?"

"Well, I watched this skinny old guy crawling through these cramped, dank, dark, incredibly small spaces to connect wires, and I thought, why not have dachshunds do it?"

"Dachshunds do it," Angelica repeated breathily. Dirk blushed.

"Yes," he replied shakily, "dachshunds could be trained to run wiring under homes and through crawl spaces. All you'd need would be an open can of dog food at one end of the passage."

"So what happened?"

"Well," Dirk said ruefully, "I was told it wouldn't pay. There is apparently a surplus of skinny old men who will happily slither through tunnels for half a can of dog food, or preferably a glass of Ripple. Unlike dachshunds, they don't have a union."

"Dachshunds have a union?"

"Yep, three actually. There's DOL, the Dachshunds Organization

League; DAG, the Dogs Actors' Guild; and TAG, the Tiny Actors' Guild. There's the Electricians' Union too, of course, but there's no Emaciated Old Alcoholics' Union, so they are easier to work with than canines."

Dirk absently stroked the curve of Angelica's hip. "Then there was my 'A diamond is forever' idea … Did you know that anything containing carbon can be turned into a diamond? All you need is intense heat and pressure. They were making diamonds out of peanut butter in Silicon Valley, just to prove the point. Well, humans contain carbon. What if, instead of burying the dead, we placed them in hot pressure chambers and diamonized them? It would free up a ton of real estate, and when a man gives the girl of his dreams a ring, it would not just be his great-grandmother's ring; it would actually be his great-grandmother. Big families would be an asset. I've even conceived of the copy: 'A Diamond is forever—shouldn't your aunt Sadie be too?'"

"You nut," Angelica moaned. She gently ruffled Dirk's hair and as he turned his face toward hers, the slow dance of love, sex, or whatever it was began all over again.

The Message

*I may not have gone where I intended to go, but I think I have
ended up where I intended to be.* —Douglas Adams

"I'm Marlene Dietrich's voice trapped in Madeline Albright's body,"
Angelica said as they lay in bed together one Friday, cradled in each
other's arms.

"Angelica, you're not that bad."

"Of course I'm not that bad, I'm in advertising. I exaggerate. What
do you expect?"

"You're beautiful, really," Dirk said, a bit awkwardly. Unschooled in
the language of love, he wasn't used to giving endearments.

Their conversation was interrupted by a postcard that flew through
the transom, into the bedroom, hitting Dirk squarely on the nose.

"What the—!" Angelica exclaimed.

Dirk hastily glanced down, "It's from my boss."

"Marcus?"

"No, my other boss. I … kind of … freelance."

He had looked at the note long enough to read: YOU ARE WAY
BEHIND DEADLINE. NO PUN INTENDED.

A second card found its way into the bedroom with the missive:
CALL ME IMMEDIATELY. 1-666-ALL-EVIL.

"I have to call my boss," Dirk said, blindly reaching for his robe.
"Excuse me for just a minute."

"That's quite some delivery service he's got," Angelica remarked. Dirk
pocketed the cards and closed the door behind him.

Lucifer answered the phone before it rang.

"It's not easy to arrange these trips, you know," he whined. "I can't have you not providing proofs on schedule. The Catholics and Calvinists will think we're not seriously recruiting. The Jews aren't so uptight—after all, it took them four centuries to write the Talmud. But I don't have four centuries! We need to get moving on the publication."

"I'm sorry," Dirk replied, not feeling at all sorry, "but this schedule is just too much! I can't keep it up."

"Perhaps if you were less interested in keeping it up ..." Lucifer let the sentence dangle menacingly.

"How do you know—? Oh, never mind," Dirk sighed. "My schedule is awful. I'm not getting enough sleep. I have no time to write my guidebook. It's gotten so that I don't even remember if I was at work or in Heaven on Thursday."

"Hmm," Lucifer said, checking his notes, "You were underground in the Egyptian afterlife. It takes a lot of people that way."

"So," Lucifer continued, with a return to the smooth, cajoling sales manner he affected whenever he wanted something, "How would you like to quit your day job? Work full-time for me?"

"What are the hours?"

"Let's say three afterlives, visited and critiqued, per week? What do you make at Pesky, Pesky & Pesky, Inc.?"

Dirk, hesitated. He made $50K a year, but perhaps he should say $70K? On the other hand, this was the Devil he was talking to ...

"How about $100K a year, plus expenses?" asked Lucifer.

Dirk was shocked into silence.

"Not enough?" the Devil queried. "Tell you what: let's make it an even $150K, but no more missing deadlines."

"Done," Dirk replied quickly. Before he could say anything more, he heard the monotonous drone of a dial tone. Too late, Dirk realized he had not asked Lucifer to explain the time disparity between Heaven and Earth, or to provide him with some sort of departure schedule.

Thus began Dirk Quigby's new career.

★

Dirk did not quite know how to tell Angelica about his new job. Just how do you inform your lover (or anyone, for that matter) that you are writing guidebooks for the Devil? Dirk decided that half a truth was better than none. He told Angelica he had managed to land a position as a writer for heavenly vacations. Angelica congratulated him with her usual conjugal enthusiasm.

"Will you be traveling?"

"Uh ... yes, but I don't have a schedule yet," Dirk replied, nervous she might want to accompany him to some Heavenly resort. "I'm not sure where I'll be going, or when."

"Travel," Angelica mused. "People say it broadens the mind, but that's not always true. It can just as easily confirm perceptions or strengthen prejudices. Sometimes it even gives rise to new ones. In Mostar, for instance, did you know they serve mayonnaise on pizza? Not just a dab either, but a huge hulking glob, right in the middle. It looks like an enormous bird just flew over your lunch. I tell you, I can never feel at home in a culture that would do that to a pizza."

"Mostar ... isn't that in Bosnia, or Croatia, one of those places where the Christians went crazy and massacred all the Muslims? Christians slaughtering Muslims—sounds like a reversal of current trends, although hardly a refreshing one. What the hell were you doing there?"

"Hell had nothing to do with it," Anglican sniffed. "Work took me there."

"Voice-overs without borders?"

Angelica laughed, "The massacres weren't about religion, not really. They were about real estate, real estate lost during the 1400s or there

47

about. The land, which had once been Bosnian, became the Ottoman empire, the Austrian empire, the Kingdom of Yugoslavia, and finally Tito's Soviet-inspired Yugoslavia. During Tito's reign, everyone was oppressed. No one was free to pursue life, liberty, and the destruction of one's neighbors. After the Soviet empire collapsed, all were once again free to persecute and massacre all those they'd hated for centuries."

"Surely that's rather cynical, isn't it?"

"It's amazing how often cynicism and reality converge."

"So what were you doing over there?"

"Oh, just looking out for some local advertisers ... But now it's you who will be traveling." She playfully circled his nipples with elegant fingers. "You were so underutilized at that Pesky place. You needed to break outside the box, my darling, and now you have!"

Dirk reached over. "I want you in my drinking water," he mumbled, covering her mouth with his.

Heaven Schmeaven

There is the fear that there is an afterlife but no one will know where it's being held. —Woody Allen

Dirk was miserable; he had a horrid attack of hay fever. His eyes were red and itchy; his nose was either completely blocked or continually dripping. He sat on the edge of the bathtub, some of Angelica's underwear (which hung over the shower curtain rod) drizzling on his head. The underwear was lacy, skimpy, and colorful, reminding Dirk of the plastic flags so popular in used-car lots.

Dirk sniffed, "One of the times in my life when I'd rather have Kleenex than sex."

Dirk reached for a tissue. His fingers grasped the soft, pliant paper, and the soft pliant paper grabbed back. Relentlessly, he was pulled toward the box. The last thing he remembered was gazing up through the clear plastic flaps that covered the opening.

When he awoke, he was on the outskirts of a small, quaint village.

DIRK QUIGBY'S GUIDE TO THE JEWISH AFTERLIFE

Notes: Judaism was one of the first monotheistic faiths, about this there is no debate. This seems to be nearly the only fact that offers no substance for dispute. These folks like to haggle. They are in continual discussion: "Who is a Jew?", "What makes a Jew?", "Can one become a Jew?", "Is Judaism a race, culture, ethnicity, or religion?" Et cetera.

END DESTINATION:

There is a lot of argument over whether or not there is an

afterlife, let alone a Heaven. And Heaven is scarcely populated because, as the majority of Jews figure that Heaven doesn't exist, most don't bother to come.

Heaven (if it actually exists) is a pleasant garden. Here, good people of all faiths (or no faith) are welcome. Rabbis are available 24/6. Hell (if there is a Hell) would not entail eternal punishment because, all evidence to the contrary, God is not a sadist.

You will be judged for your sins (if there is a judgment), but nothing—not even diamonds or damnation—is forever.

Reform Jews who believe in Heaven think that the soul alone is resurrected.

Orthodox Jews who believe in Heaven believe in the resurrection of both body and soul.

Debate continues in the afterlife. Those who are just souls argue that they are nonliving proof that only the soul survives. The bodies present themselves as material evidence to the contrary. I found the debate disconcerting, but no one else seemed bothered.

Entry Requirements:

You can always convert. Although if you are an uncircumcised male, I would not recommend it. On the other hand, if your mother is a Jew, you do not have a lot of choice.

Jews have no creed, or catechism. Individual rabbis, congregations, or movements have sometimes agreed *for as long as five minutes at a stretch* upon a dogma, but because there is no central authority, no creed takes precedence. Still, below are some basics:

God is totally powerful and all-knowing. Don't say His name or He'll be really, really angry.

Pray directly to God. Adam, Noah, and Abraham all spoke directly to God. Only *that wimp* Moses was taught via a burning bush—and look where it led him, wandering around in the desert in circles for forty years, *covering an area about the size of Palm Springs.*

After creating the world, God established a covenant with the Jewish people. He revealed His laws and commandments to them; in exchange, the Jews gave him the tips of their male babies' genitals. This is known as *Brit milah* or "Welcome to the Covenant."

Moses was given two guides on Mount Sinai. The *Torah*, or the written law, consists of the first five books of the Bible, namely Genesis through Deuteronomy.

Moses was also given an oral law, but we don't have the text. The notes, however, were eventually edited together into the *Mishnah*, which after four centuries of wrangling, became known as the *Talmud*.

The Torah, the Mishnah, and Talmud are all products of divine revelation. Although how revelation works, and what precisely one means when one says that a book is "divine," has always been a matter for dispute.

Still, the words of the prophets are true, *and written on the subway walls.*

The Torah is the primary text of Judaism. Jews are often called the "People of the Book," *even though many have branched out into television and cinema.*

There are 613 commandments in the Torah, but you have to follow only a few, since many laws were applicable only when the Temple in Jerusalem existed, but it was destroyed—and don't you forget it.

The soul is pure at birth. You have free will. You can atone for sins through prayer, repentance, and *tzedakah* (charity). God will reward those who observe His commandments and punish those who violate them.

Eventually a *moshiach* (messiah), or a messianic era, will arrive. We're not sure exactly what or when, but it's coming, so look pious.

There are three daily prayers. All services contain nineteen benedictions called the *Amidah* or the *Shemonah Esrei* ("The Eighteen"). *And these people are supposed to be good at math?* You can pray alone, but to have a service you need ten men (a *minyan*), or in the case of reformers, ten people (a *wominyan*). *If my Biblical recollections are correct, sheep were often used to make up a quorum, which seems like cheating.* There are prayers before eating (the *Hamotzi*), drinking (the *Kiddush*), and complaining (the *Kvetch*).

A lot of props are used during benedictions. There is a prayer shawl (a *tallit*), a beanie (a *yarmulke*) and, for the very observant, two leather boxes, worn on the arm (*shel yad*), and the head (*shel rosh*). These are called *tefillin*—*though not to their face.*

To be kosher, consult Leviticus, *a prospect that ought to be enough to dissuade anyone.* Don't eat predators, crustaceans, fish without scales, animals that feed on excretion, *or lawyers.* Buy two sets of crockery, one for meat, and one for milk. Mixing the two is not allowed. This avoids eating food with negative vibes. Such vibes occur when cooking a calf in its mother's milk. *French Jews have a hell of a time.*

As in all things Jewish, costumes and prayers differ widely.

The Sabbath, or *Shabbat*, is sundown Friday to sundown Saturday, and it does double duty, commemorating God's completion of Creation as well as the Exodus from Egypt. At the beginning of Shabbat, light a pair of candles and praise God. *"You look especially lovely tonight God and I promise never, ever to say your name."*

During Shabbat, you mustn't do any work, not even turn on a light switch. This is because once upon a time in a shtetel (village) far, far way, there was no such thing as electricity. To get light you had to make a fire; making a fire is work, and it's wrong to work on the Shabbat. Now good Jews put their lights on timers, or get goyim to turn on the lights … *(Try www.goyboys.com.)*

Rosh Hashanah ("Day of Remembrance") is the Jewish New Year; it falls on the first day of the seventh month. *Go figure.* The New Year celebrates the day that God created Earth. *What God was up to during the previous six months remains a mystery.* New Year's is not fun. You sit in temple (schul) wishing for "another year in the Book of Life," and repent, repent, repent. When you are finished, you repent some more. You apologize to everyone for everything. After ten days of this, you get Yom Kippur, the "Day of Atonement." You fast and pray for sins, communal as well as individual, committed during the previous year.

There are numerous minor holidays as well. Purim celebrates the time a babe named Esther saved the Jews from extermination by asking her husband not to kill them. Hanukkah, *created so little Jewish kids wouldn't feel left out at Christmas,* celebrates the Miracle of the Oil, which burned for seven days instead of one. It commemorates the Maccabees, who led a successful rebellion against the Seleucid Empire *and created the longest-burning tallow on the market.* During Hanukkah, *which has more spellings than Muhammad or Al Qaeda,* you should eat fried foods to celebrate the inexpugnable oil, *and pray for low cholesterol.*

QUALITY RATINGS:
Perks: ★★ —If you enjoy continual Talmudic discussion, I recommend this Heaven.

You don't have to go to church on Sunday.

Food: ★★★ —Kosher, of course. Like gefilte fish and unleavened bread? However, you can get a damn good hot pastrami on rye, and this is definitely number one for pickles.

Drink: ★ ★ —If you have a sweet tooth, you'll love it. *Connoisseurs have been known to sneak into the Catholics' heavenly wine cellar.*

Music: ★ ★ —Klezmer, schmezmer. Rock out to popular tunes like: "Baklava (the Middle Eastern Treat)," and "Thirteen Turned the Boy," oy vey!

Accommodations: ★ ★ ★ —Simple and clean.

Entry Requirements: ★ ★ ★ ★

OVERALL RATING: ★ ★ ★

Dirk awoke on his couch, his mind reeling from the endless discussions, diatribes, and debates the Jews seemed to live (or perhaps die) for. He looked at the clock, then checked his computer. According to them, he had been in heaven for fifteen minutes. Once again, his wristwatch disagreed. It claimed he had been away for three days.

Endings and Beginnings

Life is pleasant. Death is peaceful. It's the
transition that's troublesome. —Isaac Asimov

Notes:
There are so many kinds of Jews! Orthodox Jews believe that God dictated
the Torah directly to Moses, who was better with stenography than direc-
tions. The Torah's laws are binding, unchanging and exceedingly picayune.
Modern Orthodoxy is more modern, yet still orthodox.
Haredi is sometimes referred to as Ultra-Orthodox, but only by people
who don't like it. Haredi, means "fear" or "anxiety," oy vey.
Conservative Jews believe that the Torah was inspired but not actually
dictated by God. Maybe they figure God was busy off creating something
at the time.
Progressive Judaism is less progressive than Reform Judaism.
Reconstructionist Judaism is philosophical.
And Humanistic Judaism is a nonreligious movement that celebrates folk
dancing and potato pancakes (latkes).

Dirk made his final trip into Pesky, Pesky, & Pesky, Inc. on Friday.

"I need to talk to you," he said, poking his head into Marcus's office.

"Come in, come in," Marcus said genially.

It appeared that Dirk was not the only one to be enticed by Angelica. Since the frog had taken up residence in her throat, campaigns were hopping! The Voice could sell anything.

"I quit," Dirk said without preamble.

"Wait just a minute, pal," Marcus snapped. "You're on contract here, okaaay? You can't just quit."

"Nevertheless, I do."

"Let's talk this over, okaaay? No point in being hasty, now. You've been doing wonderful work lately. Really getting it ..."

"Glad to have made you happy. I quit."

"Perhaps you've received a better offer?" Marcus asked, narrowing his eyes.

"Perhaps I have."

"Well," Marcus said heartily, slapping Dirk on the back, "that can be dealt with. How much did they offer you?"

"A hundred-fifty K plus expenses and lots of travel perks."

Marcus was silent.

"That's a lot of money," he admitted. "I doubt we could match that, but Dirk, you've worked here fifteen years! You're part of our happy family! A business partnership is more than just cash, it's like a marriage."

"Then I want a divorce."

"Who are you planning to work for?"

"You wouldn't believe me if I told you."

"Try me."

"The Devil."

There was a moment's silence. Then Marcus burst out in a hearty laugh, "Aren't we all, Dirk, aren't we all ... still, better the devil you know ..." He let the sentence dangle enticingly.

"Sorry," said Dirk, who wasn't sorry. "It's a once-in-a-lifetime offer; I'm taking it."

"Don't come begging to me if it doesn't work out, okaaay?" Marcus growled, affability vanishing. "You're not cut out for the big time. You show up late, looking like something the cat dragged in. Before you know it you'll be out on your ear."

Dirk watched in fascination as Marcus got red, agitated, and foamy, resembling beet juice in a blender.

"Just don't come crying to me if you mess this up. I won't take you back, and with an attitude like yours, you'll never work in this town again."

"This town isn't where I plan to be working," Dirk replied calmly. "Good-bye, Marcus," he said, extending his hand, but Marcus ignored it.

"Have a nice life, okaaay?" Dirk said. He turned away, happily closing the door on what had been his reality for fifteen years.

The Six Ages of Man

Oh, East is East and West is West, and never the twain shall meet,
till Earth and Sky stand presently at God's great Judgment Seat.
—Rudyard Kipling

Dirk felt light. It was a glorious spring day. After fifteen years, his pesky shackles had been severed. He was traveling, writing, and best of all, there was an afterlife.

Granted, it was not the quite the enlightened, mind-altering place he had imagined, but at least it existed. That meant death was not final; even the worst heaven beat the hell out of nonexistence. His mood was further enhanced by the husky voice of Angelica.

Dirk felt as though he had awakened from a ten-year hibernation. During his servitude at Pesky, Pesky, & Pesky, Inc., he had gradually ceased activities that gave him pleasure. He had stopped bicycling, never went to concerts, clubs, or movies. He had even stopped dating. Indeed his only social contact had been the forced congeniality of work. Although he'd always liked Angelica, he'd never seen her outside of the office. Now she was his world.

It struck him that he had been trying to punish life for its lack of meaning by curtailing his existence. He had protested the loss of his dreams by depriving himself of pleasure. But now that would change.

Comparative religion with Lucifer beats psychoanalysis—an hour with Satan verses years of therapy: 'Fiend Fixes Freud,' 'Incubus Ousts Introspection,' 'Beelzebub Beats Behavior Modification.'" Dirk had gotten into the habit of thinking in slogans.

He decided to do something he had not done for a long, long time—bicycling. Humming tunelessly, he went to the garage and removed his bike from its covering of dust. It had been sadly ignored and was shrouded in cobwebs.

It looks, thought Dirk, *like Miss Havisham's bicycle would have looked, if she had had one.*

Dirk cleaned it off and retrieved an ancient red metal foot pump. Assuming that the domed shape of the tires was due to neglect rather than holes, he screwed on the nozzle and, planting both feet on the foot stand, began to pump.

By the time he had finished the first tire, Dirk was sweating. He almost decided to shelve the ride, but after a brief rest, he revived.

Attaching nozzle to nipple, he began to pump again. His efforts were either too weak or the rear tire had a leak, because the tire remained the shape of an umbrella. Dirk paused; he listened, then decided to submerge the wheel in water to test for a leak. When he unscrewed the pump, a powerful jet of air yanked his finger to the nozzle. In horror, he tried to pull his hand free, but to no avail. He was relentlessly sucked, stretched, lengthened, and inhaled into encasing darkness.

DIRK QUIGBY'S GUIDE TO THE JAIN AFTERLIFE

END DESTINATION:

As with many of the Eastern afterlives I visited, there is no *there* there. One does the best one can in this life to gain a favorable reincarnation in the next life. If you are really, really good, you may get to *moksha* and become part of the great nothingness. *I'm not nearly pure enough to find comfort in this.*

ENTRY REQUIREMENTS:

The universe was never created, nor will it ever cease. It is eternal, passing through an endless series of cycles. Each cycle is divided into six ages (*Yugas*) that last thousands of years. We are currently in the fifth age. It's described as "wholly evil. Men live no longer than 125 years" *and that's a generous estimate.* If you think things are lousy now, just wait till the sixth epoch! Then, "man's life span will be sixteen to twenty years, and his height will be reduced to that of a dwarf."

During the sixth age, even Jainism will be lost. But don't worry, be happy—the cycle begins again. "In the first era, man's needs will be fulfilled by wishing trees. Man's height will be six miles, and evil will be unknown," *although headroom might be a problem.*

Reality is made up of two eternal principles, *jiva* and *ajiva*. Jiva is soul, and ajiva is matter, motion, space, and time. Both are eternal. The whole world consists of jivas trapped in ajiva; there are jivas in rocks, plants, insects, animals, human beings, spirits, and even lawyers.

Any contact with the ajiva causes the jiva to suffer. Suffer, suffer, suffer. *It's as though the ajiva is forcing the jiva to down a case of tiramisu cakes and try on bikinis in a room filled with supermodels.* Existence means suffering: agony, anguish, deterioration, and wretchedness. Not social reform, nor individual rectification can ease the misery.

The only way to escape is for the jiva to completely break away from the four *ghatis* (stages) of existence: Human life, Heavenly bodies, Sentient creatures (Plants/Animals/Insects/Fish), and Hell. The only way to escape these is to practice Jainism continuously.

Any and every action stimulates the senses. Then *karma*, an invisible substance, *I think it's a gas,* seeps in and adheres to the jiva, weighing it down and determining its next incarnation. Evil actions create heavy karma, and force it to enter life at a lower level *such as a naked mole rat, grub, or politician.* Good deeds, on the other hand, create light karma, and allow the jiva to rise to a higher level, where there is less suffering. *Paris Hilton was a fabulous squid in her last incarnation.* Good deeds, however, can never lead to release. The way to reach moksha and cease to exist, *a goal I always have trouble relating to,* is to close off your senses and mind, thus preventing karmic matter from entering and adhering to your jiva.

With no karma to weigh it down at death, the jiva will float free of all ajiva, free of the human condition, free of all future embodiments. It will rise to the top of the universe (*Siddhashila*). There, the jiva, identical to all other pure jivas, will experience eternal stillness, isolation, noninvolvement, and finally, moksha—*the great nothingness where you can hang out with other successful mokska-oriented jivas such as Buddhists and Hindus, or rather you could hang out with them if they still existed.*

In order to ensure a favorable next life, or if you're really lucky, totally cease to exist, one must follow the three jewels—knowledge, right faith, and right conduct. The fundamental principal is *ahimsa*, or respect for all life, *including life that goes out of its way not to be respected, such as mosquitoes, lice, ticks, bedbugs, or leeches.* Monks and nuns wear veils covering their mouths and nostrils to prevent inhaling insects, and carry a brush to sweep bugs out of harm's way.

There are the two main sects of Jain monks. The Digambar monks do not wear any clothes because they believe that clothes are possessions, and possessions increase desire. *One might suppose that a lot of nude monks wandering around could increase desire, but not on their diet. Besides they're short.* The Digambar believe that women cannot attain moksha, *possibly because they insist on wearing clothes, the hussies!* They also believe that none of the Jain religious texts are totally authentic.

The Svetambar monks wear white, unstitched, cotton clothes, *condemning only plaids and polyester.* Svetambars believe that women can attain moksha. They also believe there are unaltered religious texts.

The *sadhvis* (women) of both sects wear white clothes, *and believe that they would be better off without all these naked monks and religious texts.*

All Jains are vegetarians—vegetarians who don't kill either animal or plant. Thus, they eat only leaves, fruits, and nuts. Forget about steak or carrots; both kill the Source.

Monks and nuns follow five vows: Ahimsa—nonviolence; Satya—truth telling; Asteya—not stealing; Aparigraha—renouncing possessions; and Brahmacharya—chastity. Then there's also some minor stuff, like not eating cooked food and not eating after dark … in fact eating is to be avoided whenever possible. The Jain diet plan makes following the vow of chastity easy.

All of the festivals last one day, except Paryusana, which lasts eight days. For Paryusana, everyone follows the rules of conduct as strictly as the monks and nuns. They confess their sins and reconcile with enemies and relatives. *I thought it interesting that relatives and enemies were lumped together.* And of course they must fast. *Sounds like a hell of a festival!*

Jains can pursue only nonviolent professions. Banking is tolerable, but farming is unacceptable, because you might kill a bug. *Obviously, these people have never met any serious bankers.*

The best, holiest way to die, and perhaps (if you are really, really lucky) attain nothingness, is Sallekhana. Now what, you may wonder, would Jains consider the holiest way to die? You guessed it: ritual self-starvation!

After a visit to this way station between lives, I began to see the appeal of nothingness.

QUALITY RATINGS:

Perks: ★ —*You never have to separate colors from whites when washing.*

You'll never get trichinosis.

Food: ★ —Campbell's Cream of Nothing Soup

Drink: ★ —See Food.

Music: ★ —With any luck, the meager diet will have dulled your hearing.

Accommodations: ★ —Like nothingness?

Entry Requirements: ★

OVERALL RATING: ★

As usual, Dirk returned to his plaid couch, and as usual, had been gone far longer than he had been gone. It seemed like eternity. He was hungry, thirsty, horny, and covered in welts. He wanted to eat, drink, fornicate, and commit genocide upon any insect with a mouth. "So much for purity," he grumbled, making a beeline for the refrigerator.

"So what do you think?" Lucifer asked.

Dirk started, then replied, "I can't help noticing, that time is unpredictable in Heaven. I can be gone for five days, and sometimes only a few minutes have passed on Earth. Other times, I might be gone only a day, yet three or four hours have passed on Earth."

"Ahh," Lucifer sighed, spreading out his magnificent hands. Frowning at his little finger, he pulled out a small silver file. "Time," he said, carefully shaping the offending nail, "is relative. A weekend with a friend is over before you know it, but half an hour in the Department of Motor Vehicles lasts forever. Heaven is like that. If you're lying on a couch being pleasured by a lovely woman, time is bound to pass faster than if you are kneeling on wooden floorboards offering 'thanks be to Jesus' that you have made it to Heaven."

"Yes, I know time seems relative, but—"

"On Earth," Lucifer interrupted, pocketing his file, "time seems relative; in Heaven, time *is* relative."

"It certainly makes planning difficult."

"You are not the first to be inconvenienced by an unexpected trip to the afterlife. Get used to it."

"The time of Dirk's going is never foretold," Dirk, intoned, "and the hour of Dirk's return is never revealed. I never can remember returning, you know. And going is always unexpected and extremely unpleasant. I'm beginning to be fearful of opening a can or reaching for a tissue. I never know when I'll go, and I never know where I'll end up."

"None of us does," Lucifer replied.

"Yes, but most folks don't experience death by bicycle pump, get turned into mini-tornados, or sucked into tissue boxes on a regular basis."

"Most folks," Lucifer replied in an injured tone, "don't get frequent-flyer round trips to Heaven. It's not easy arranging all this, you know. The reason you never remember returning to Earth is that it's never been done. You, Dirk Quigby," Lucifer said, dramatically opening his arms wide, "are the first. How are we supposed to know what a return from death is like? Very few have done it."

"What do you mean, 'very few'?"

"Well, Lazarus, but he never went very far, so that was easy. Christ, of course, but he returned to a cave. It was dark; we didn't have to worry about visuals. But you, Dirk, are returning regularly and returning unaltered, at least physically; it's a first."

"I always seem to return to an overstuffed, slightly dirty couch."

"Well, what could be more reassuring than that?" Lucifer grinned, patting him on the back, "It guarantees a soft landing, and it's immediately apparent that you aren't in Heaven. None of the afterlives have furniture like this."

"More fools they," Dirk sighed, leaning back into soft, voluptuous plaid.

Three in One

Angelica was coming over. Dirk was preparing a romantic dinner. Cooking was not his forte, but armed with a timer and *The Joy of Cooking*, he was making what he hoped would be a delicious dinner. The ingredients were fresh. Angelica had a taste for spice, so he'd made a special trip to the farmers' market for extra-hot peppers. Dirk chopped and diced. After dinner, they would make love. They'd wake in the morning to make love again, have a late breakfast, and then … the possibilities were limitless. Dirk sighed in contented anticipation. It was almost time for her arrival. He rushed to the bathroom.

Unfortunately, he did not wash his hands prior to relieving himself. When Angelica softly knocked on the door, she heard anguished cries emanating from the bathroom.

"What's wrong?" she cried, rushing inside to the bathroom door.

"Ahhhh," Dirk screamed, "I was cutting peppers and I had to pee." He began cursing violently.

"R-r-run it under water," Angelica snorted.

"Are you laughing?" Dirk cried in outrage, "I'm in pain here."

"N-n-no, darling," Angelica giggled. "Of course not, I'm so sorry, you're in pain, but you have to admit—"

Whatever Dirk had to admit, he could not hear, because he was holding his throbbing organ under a cooling stream of water. Then Dirk felt a tug. "No," he wailed, "not with my pants down." But either no one was listening or no one cared, for before Dirk could zip up his pants, he was tugged, penis-first, into the tap.

Dirk awoke, pants down, outside a pair of giant austere wrought-iron gates. These were manned, or perhaps angeled, by elongated figures in red robes. They had Modigliani faces and silver wings. They looked at Dirk with lofty disdain.

DIRK QUIGBY'S GUIDE
TO THE ROMAN CATHOLIC AFTERLIFE

Note: There are two regions in this Heaven. The new section has kinder, gentler requirements than the old. But this newer, more merciful and forgiving dogma has, by and large, yet to trickle down to Earth.

END DESTINATION:

Heaven (by way of Purgatory) a glorious garden, or Hell, a fiery wasteland.

In Heaven, I was given a superb new body. Although only a beige standard issue, I could float above clouds. I looked gorgeous. In fact, because God is perfection, I looked like God. Everybody looked like God. I saw Mr. McCracken, my eighth-grade gym teacher who moved here after twenty years in Purgatory.

Non-Catholics are damned and will burn in Hell forever.

There won't be any close friendships or marriages, because all and sundry will be on cloud nine just to be near God. It's like being on a date with your favorite rock star.

LIMBO AND PURGATORY:

In the old region, Purgatory is a place of torment and hellfire, where all—even the popes, nuns, and priests, *well, of course priests*—must spend varied amounts of time to expiate their sins before they are allowed entry into Heaven.

In the new section, Purgatory is a "condition" rather than a place of transition. Hard luck for those early Christians who spent a hell of a long time burning there.

Most of the kinder facets *of the new theology* have not yet become popular, so churches are still full of the faithful saying prayers, rosary, and lighting candles to lessen Purgatory time for their loved ones.

Limbo was originally a place between Heaven and Hell for the unbaptized, mostly infants and idiots, who had not had the time or brains to sin. It was also home to those great figures (Homer, Moses, etc.) who could not believe in and accept Jesus as their savior because he hadn't been born. Also in limbo were all those folks who would gladly and fervently have accepted Jesus as their savior, but due to time, distance, or lack of education, had never heard of him. *No Heaven for you.*

Limbo, however, is now in foreclosure. The Church is concerned that the concept of Limbo may not be popular with potential converts, especially in Third World countries that are crawling with dead babies.

If I was one of those infants and idiots who spent thousands of years wandering around Limbo before being allowed into Heaven and given a spiffy new body, I would be peeved, to say the least. Luckily, being infants and idiots, they aren't smart enough to be angry. They have fabulous bodies, but not many brains. There is a hot competition between the Pentecostals and the Roman Catholics as to who can gather the most infants and idiots into Heaven.

ENTRY REQUIREMENTS:

Believe in at least one incident of virgin birth by a higher mammal.

If you are a scientist or a mathematician, this is probably not the afterlife for you: not only do these people have a long history of opposing astronomy, evolution, and genetics, they also appear to be arithmetically challenged:

For there is one Person of the Father, another of the Son, and another of the Holy Ghost ... and yet they are not three but one.

This, the Athanasian Creed, provides the "clearest definitions of the Mysteries of the Trinity." *The authors of this creed are now busily at work on the tax code.*

Go to confession (the sacrament of Penance). No need to confess sins committed prior to baptism, because baptism wipes the slate clean. Of course, as Catholics are baptized in infancy, the only sin they are guilty of is original sin, which they had nothing to do with *unless they were extremely precocious.*

Catholics believe that no man, be he priest *or be he nun,* has the power to forgive sins, *except ones involving young boys;* however, once in the confessional, God possesses the priest *in a good way.* The priest is judge and jury, *and often, during crusades and inquisitions, the executioner.*

If you do not confess your mortal sins before dying, you will go straight to Hell *without dinner.* You may confess venial sins if you want to. "A person who frequently indulges in venial sin is very likely to collapse into mortal sin." *These are the same theologians who produced the film "Reefer Madness."*

The confessional has not changed for centuries, although at one time confessions were public. Prior to Vatican II, the priest would absolve the penitent in Latin, *so the penitent was never certain if he was absolved or not.*

The big difference between mortal and venial sins is that mortal sins cannot be accidental. A person who knows that their sin is wrong but commits it anyway is guilty, guilty, guilty. *When asked, "Does this make me look fat?" prepare to burn.*

Canon law requires you to confess at least once a year, although more frequent confession is advised. *Kind of like wearing clean underwear just in case you get hit by a car.* Confidentiality of confession is absolute.

If you are an adult and want to convert, it takes time.

First, is The Period of Inquiry *not to be confused with the period of inquisition.* Next phase, you need to write a letter saying why you want to convert *and what you did on your summer vacation.*

Second: the Period of the Catechumen. Accept Jesus Christ as your savior and go to Mass.

During the Eucharist, also known as Communion, sip wine and eat communion wafers, which taste suspiciously like cardboard. The word *Eucharist* comes from the Greek noun *thanksgiving as in, "I give thanks that I don't have to eat more than one of these."*

The bread and wine are consecrated—one chomp and the wafers mysteriously transform into Christ's body. "Their appearance does not change, but their substance does." This is known as transubstantiation. "The Eucharist is not a representation, but an actual participation in the Sacrifice of Christ; the only difference is in the manner in which it is offered." *One involves nails, the other the mastication of cardboard. It's hard to believe that these are the same folks who get so upset about witchcraft.* Eucharist marks full membership in the Church.

Because it's so important, I wanted to provide a catalogue of mortal sins, but there were just too many. Of course, there are the biggies: Murder, Rape, Thievery, Adultery, Incest, Fornication, *Polka Music,* Terrorism, Abortion, Homosexuality, and Sodomy. However, there are a host of others that I never imagined would make you burn for all eternity. *That God guy sure can hold a grudge.* Also not popular with the Heavenly Host are Euthanasia, Suicide, Scandal, Drug Abuse, and Gluttony. *There goes Rush Limbaugh on at least three counts.* Beware of Artificial Birth Control, Extreme Anger, Divorce, and Masturbation. *There goes the St. Francis Boys' Academy.* Eschew Cheating, Unfair Wagers, Alcohol Abuse, and Adulation (speech or an attitude that encourages others to be naughty). Don't Covet Your Neighbor's Wife (*No worries there, God's obviously never seen her*), and a score more.

Suffice it to say, if you in any way, shape, or form disrespect God or the Church, either by Luke Warmness, Doubt, Presuming that You Can Save Yourself, or That God Will Save You Without Repentance and Conversion, you will fry.

The Catholic Church is the only true church of Jesus Christ.

The pope is God's mouthpiece on Earth; he is infallible. *This made for some very tense moments in Heaven when a number of God's mouthpieces were having dinner together. I witnessed some infallibly vehement disagreements.*

QUALITY RATINGS:
Perks: ★★ —Confession is a rather handy way to obtain forgiveness without apologizing.

If you enjoy pomp, circumstance, authority figures, and being perpetually confused, this may be your heaven. Mass, though no longer conducted in Latin, might as well be, as nobody really understands what's being said. All the authority figures wear interesting, colorful costumes—from nuns, to bishops, to the pope. This makes it easy to recognize them and obey.

Music: ★★★ —From Gregorian chant to the *Messiah* and *Ave Maria* ... if you like classical music, this is the place for you!

Food: ★★★ —It's a fabulous banquet.

Drink: ★ ★ ★ ★ —Catholics have a long history of viticulture and it doesn't end with this life.
Accommodations: ★ ★ ★ ★ ★ —It's a fabulous garden.
Entry Requirements:
　　New Region: ★ ★ ★
　　Old Region: ★ ★
OVERALL RATING: ★ ★

Thanks to the time difference, Dirk was absent from his apartment for only two minutes, although he was in Heaven for three days. Landing on the couch, he was greeted by an incessant drumming: Angelica pounding on the bathroom door.

"Are you all right?" she called. "I'm really sorry I laughed at you. I know it must hurt—why don't you come out, so I can kiss it and make it better?"

Thinking quickly, Dirk snuck up behind her and covered her eyes. "Boo," he whispered.

Angelica shrieked and leaped into the air, attaining an elevation that would have made Nureyev envious, especially as he is dead.

"*Ahhhhhh*," she yelled her honeyed voice harsh. "Where were you? How the hell did you get out of the bathroom?"

"Hell," Dirk said, kissing her, "had nothing to do with it. There's a secret passage."

"Show me," she demanded.

"Later. Right now, let's enjoy this lovely dinner, before it gets cold."

Although Angelica was by no means satisfied, she allowed herself to be coaxed to the table. There Dirk plied her with spices and alcohol, hoping to make her forget the mysterious passage.

Revelation

Between lovers, a little confession is a dangerous thing.
—Helen Rowland

Notes:
Why original sin? If everybody has it, it's not very original.
Amazingly few priests. Where are they?
If Catholics don't believe in evolution, why is the pope called the head primate?

Later that night Dirk lay in bed with Angelica, toasting his love with Pinot noir. Angelica too had left Pesky. Ever since the frog had moved in, she was in constant demand for voice-overs. She and her faithful amphibian could work as much, or as little as they wanted.

"Here's to us!" Dirk said, looking deep into her surprisingly beautiful gray-green eyes. "You really could be lovely, you know," he said, curling her admittedly stringy hair around his finger.

"Could be? Nice love talk!"

"No, truly ... it didn't come out right. I'm not used to this. I feel so completely at home with you. I can be myself for the first time in a long time, maybe forever."

"Forever's a long time."

"Longer than you know."

"Are you turning religious on me?" Angelica asked incredulously.

"Yes. I mean no ... I mean yes ... I just don't know which one yet."

"This wouldn't have anything to do with your mysterious new job now, would it?"

Dirk lay quiet, hoping she would not continue this line of conversation.

"Just what is your new job?" she pursued.

"I'm kind of starting a new project for him, uh, I mean, them. Like I told you, I'm writing guidebooks for Heavenly Vacations."

"What exactly is Heavenly Vacations? Guidebooks to where?"

"You wouldn't believe me," he said miserably.

"Try me," she raised herself up on her elbows.

And so, for the second time that day, Dirk tried.

"I work for the Devil."

"Most of us do, in one way or another, but are you doing the Devil's work? That's the important question."

"I don't know."

"Why won't you confide in me?"

"I'm trying," Dirk cried unhappily, "but Angelica, can't we just talk about something else for a while?"

"What do you want to talk about?"

"Maybe us?"

"What about us?"

"Well, I think I love you. I really trust you, sort of."

"High praise indeed!"

"I'm no good at this," Dirk acknowledged. "I've never felt like this before. I feel I've known you all my life."

"Well, maybe you have."

The Dirk of two months ago would have scoffed, but with his recent forays into Paradise and under the strain of repeatedly running into reincarnations, he had to admit that this was indeed a possibility.

"Do you believe you knew me in another life?" he asked.

"No," she replied, "I think maybe I have known you always in this one."

He rolled over to look into her naked eyes.

"I don't know how to tell you this," she purred, her aphrodisiac tones dripping honey. "I'm here to … sort of watch over you. I'm your guardian angel."

Dirk lay still, shocked into silence.

"Hey, are you okay?" Angelica asked.

"I don't know, I feel stunned. I feel shell-shocked, I feel used … I feel—Are you fucking me for my salvation?"

They looked at each other. Unable to face her, Dirk turned away.

"If you're an angel, why aren't you a lot more attractive? Is this the best you could do?"

"Would you have asked me out if I was gorgeous?" her voice, like liquid butterscotch, flowing into all the sharp corners of his being.

Ruefully, Dirk had to admit that he probably wouldn't have.

"So I'm *schtupping* an angel and working for Lucifer. My high school aptitude test never pegged me for this!"

"Well," Angelica retorted sweetly, "I didn't exactly choose to be the guardian angel of advertising myself."

"So do you fuck all your charges?"

"If all my 'charges,' as you put it, were as cute as you …" Angelica let the sentence dangle alluringly.

"Am I your first Earthling?" Dirk asked, feeling like he was in a science-fiction novel.

Angelica kissed his nose and ignored the question. "I love Earth," she said. "It's such a wonderfully diverse place—a host of divergent life forms, scores of individuals within each species. In fact, Earth species have only four things in common: they are born, eat, have sex, and die. The middle two are the most fun, and I intend to have as much as possible of both while I'm here."

Dirk liked her philosophy just fine.

Theology

Sex is one of the nine reasons for reincarnation—
the other eight are unimportant. —Henry Miller

Notes:
The Catholics have patron saints, who are special protectors over certain
areas of life. These can include occupations, illnesses, churches, countries,
or causes. Saint Francis of Assisi loved nature and so he is the patron
saint of ecologists. Clare of Assisi is the patron saint of television because
one Christmas when too ill to leave her bed, she saw and heard Christ-
mas Mass even though it was taking place miles away. Why she wasn't
named the patron Saint of LSD?
You can find a patron saint for anyone. Some of my favorites are:
African-Americans—St. Benedict the African.
Bakers—St. Elizabeth of Hungary.
Baptism—St. John the Baptist. Duh!
Brewers, bakers, and brides—St. Nicholas. Also moonlights as Santa.
Canada, China, and death—St. Joseph. Why does death need a patron
saint, and how do Canada and China feel about this?
Comedians and Epilepsy—St. Vitus. It's so funny when he has a
seizure.
Deafness—St. Francis de Sales. What?
Difficult marriages—St. Rita of Cascia. Her husband could not be found
for comment.
Dogs—St. Roch. Dogs?
Ear aches—St. Polycarp. Shouldn't he be the patron Saint of goldfish?
Europe is a big place so they have three—St. Benedict, St. Bridget, and
St. Catherine of Siena.

Why is sex considered so wrong in most religions, although it is sometimes allowed in the afterlife?

Why is the need for intercourse programmed into our very being? Why does it feel so good if it is so bad?

When Adam and Eve were innocent, being naked and having sex was fine. Once they had knowledge, it was wrong. Now this may sound blasphemous, but I'm confused … God has knowledge, so why wasn't it wrong for Him to view naked primates having intercourse?

If man is created in God's image, who does God have intercourse with?

Dirk had not actually spoken aloud, but Angelica answered him anyway.

"You will find as you visit more and more afterlives, the acceptance of sex in afterlives varies hugely from heaven to heaven. So does whether or not God (or gods, my monotheistic darling), gets to participate. The Hare Krishnas decry intercourse, but Krishna is insatiable!

"As for other species … well, they have different beliefs. If you humans are so varied in your ideas, you surely can't expect a *philodina roseola* to hold to your conception of the truth."

"What," Dirk said, raking a hand nervously through his hair, "or who, is the *philodina roseola?*"

Angelica grinned. "I thought you'd never ask," she purred throatily. "The *philodina roseola* is a bdelloid rotifer, a class of microscopic freshwater invertebrates comprising some 350 species. For the *philodina roseola*, males are unknown. She may be the only true virgin there is … her kind hasn't had sex for about eighty-five thousand years. The funny thing is, they worship sex! According to their mythology, the first *philodina roseolas* were born having sexual relations in Paradise, but after they had eaten the algae of knowledge, they were driven from Paradise and had to become sexless."

"You're kidding."

"Actually," Angelica smiled, "yes, I am kidding. But that's beside the point. Perhaps it's the nature of Earthlings to crave what they can't have: virginity and celibacy for your species, and rampant sexuality for the *philodina roseola*."

In spite of his wariness, Dirk continued to pursue his ever-deepening relationship with Angelica. He felt he had no choice. Granted, it was more than a bit unnerving to be screwing an angel, but Dirk was falling in love.

"I'm glad I'm not dating anymore," Dirk confided over a dinner of pizza, salad, and red wine (one small salad and medium pizza for Dirk; a large salad, a plate of antipasti, an order of garlic bread, and a super-giant, extra-humongous, quadruple-cheese pizza with triple toppings for Angelica). "I hated dating; it's like going on a job interview for a job you probably don't want, and having to pay for it."

"You humans think you have it bad! What about slime molds? They have over seven hundred separate sexes; can you imagine their personal ads?"

"Slimelove@sevensex.com."

"Or consider certain species of fish. Some begin life as males but mature into females, and other species change seemingly at will. When males are needed they are male, when males dominate, they morph into females. Talk about a sexual-identity crisis!

"And have you even considered whiptail lizards, aphids, or the myriad of fish species that reproduce by parthenogenesis?"

"What's parthenogenesis?" Dirk inquired cautiously, not entirely certain he wanted to know.

"Parthenogenesis, is the reproduction of an unfertilized egg—virgin birth, if you will. I always wondered if that was the reason so many Christians use fish to symbolize their religion. They are very fond of virgin birth, you know."

"True, but they aren't very fond of science. Why do you know so much about other species? Were you in on the blueprints? Or is it mandatory for guardian angels?"

Angelica smiled seductively, "Nothing, my darling, is mandatory for angels."

Their scientific discussions of sex and species culminated in a hands-on revelation.

★

Later as they lay in bed, Angelica neatly nestled into Dirk's chest, she continued: "I've always wondered, why does your species imagine itself unique? Do you suppose other genera don't have guardian angels?"

Dirk was startled, "Do they? Are animal guardian-angels animals?"

"Usually guardian angels appear to be the same species as their charges."

"Humm," Dirk mused, "I always supposed that animals might have souls, at least some of them … but guardian angels?"

Angelica laughed, "You humans are so absolute. Must all people have souls, and no animals? Isn't it just vaguely possible that some but not all humans have souls, and the same might be true for other varieties of life?"

"Are you saying some people lack souls and some animals have them?"

"Every species has certain unifying traits and characteristics. You humans, for instance, have wonderfully clever thumbs, the class Aves has wings—but individuals are individual. Bowerbirds, for example, have rather drab feathers; the males, sweet dears, try to impress potential mates by constructing fabulous bowers. They don't lay eggs in these constructions, oh no; they are strictly for lovemaking. The bowerbirds meticulously decorate and redecorate their love-nests with flowers and leaves. Their bowers face the sun and are filled with light. All male bowerbirds do this, but some bowerbirds insist on perfecting a pattern or design, even if by so doing they lose out on the chance to mate that year. Surely, that begs the case for an artistic spirit, if not a soul? And what is a soul if not the ability to create beauty?"

"Good question," Dirk said. "What is a soul?"

"I'm your guardian angel, not your guru," Angelica replied, forestalling further discussion with a kiss.

The Many Hands of God

I don't believe in reincarnation, and I didn't believe in it when I was a hamster. —Shane Ritchie

Dirk had never had much of a green thumb, but he'd never had much of a garden either. His garden consisted of a slender strip of earth that ran along the three steps leading to his front door. When he'd first moved in, he would occasionally imagine greenery or flowers brightening his entryway. Then he would rush out, purchase some plants guaranteed to be un-killable, and plop them haphazardly in the earth. At best, he watered sporadically. To his geraniums, he seemed a heedless and uncaring deity.

After fifteen years of working at Pesky, Pesky, & Pesky, Inc., Dirk had lost hope and interest in most things. This was reflected in the utter neglect of his pathetic garden. It was due only to stubborn will and indomitable DNA that a few scrawny geraniums managed to eek out an existence. Now however, Dirk had a new life. He was making a living writing, he went on frequent junkets to Paradise, and his girlfriend was an angel; it was time to care for his garden.

Smiling at the sun, Dirk unfurled the abandoned hose and turned on the water. The hose lacked a nozzle, and water gushed out in a stream so powerful it uprooted the first miserable geranium it contacted. He bent over to right the fallen flower, and gently replace it in a bed of mud. Then he inserted his finger into the hose, creating a diffuse spray. Humming happily, he sprinkled the plants with a gentle rain. Resolving to be a more faithful caretaker, Dirk reached back to turn off the hose, but his finger stuck. He jerked his finger in one direction and viciously yanked the hose in the other, but it was no use. The more he pulled, the harder the resistance. With a final vast suction from the hose, Dirk was wrung, streamlined, and elongated into a rushing torrent of darkness.

He came to consciousness in front of a blue-bodied, elephant-headed creature who was motioning him forward with its myriad arms.

Dirk Quigby's Guide to the Hindu Afterlife

In former times you had to be born Hindu. Nowadays you can convert. However, trying to memorize the variety of deities is mind-boggling. *If not begun in earliest childhood, it would be impossible. It's worse than French!* There is only one God, but he has 330 million nicknames.

A second consolation: if you were not born Hindu in this incarnation, maybe you'll get lucky in the next. Everybody goes through countless reincarnations.

End Destination:

Reincarnation, or Moksa, *sounds like a tasty kebob, but actually* means spiritual liberation leading to nonexistence. *Not much of a goal in my humble opinion.* Heaven (Svarga Loka) and Hell (Naraka Loka) are temporary.

Entry Requirements:

There are four major denominations of Hinduism: Vaishnavism, Shaivism, Shaktism, and Smartism, although many Hindus, *just to be ornery,* claim not to belong to any denomination at all.

This world is only a pleasant soul station if you are lucky enough to have been born into a high caste. You are born into a high caste only if you have good karma. It is much easier to obtain good karma if you are in a high caste. *This is called Caste-22.*

You might enjoy this heaven if you delight in chanting mantras and saying "om" a lot. *Aum* (or Om) is suffixed to all Hindu mantras and prayers. "Om" contains the primordial vibration of the Universe. A mantra is a hymn to a deity. A mantra is associated with a yantra. A yantra is a mystical diagram. All acts of worship, which include mantras and yantras, are called tantras. *Dr. Shakivism Seuss is very popular here, especially his classic children's tale, "One Mantra, Blue Yantra, Red Yantra, Two Tantras."* Tantras can be divided into two paths: the right-hand path (known as either Samayachara, or Dakshinachara— *because why use one word when you can use two?*), and the left-hand path, Vamachara.

Extolled as a shortcut to self-realization and spiritual enlightenment by some, left-hand tantric rites are often rejected as dangerous. Left-hand practice forces adherents to confront their conditioned responses by doing naughty things, such as having sex (preferably with a low-caste partner), eating meat (particularly beef and pork), and drinking alcohol. Fear is also used: the boozing, low-caste sex, and pork partying might be conducted in a cremation ground amidst decomposing corpses.

Remember that Brahman is the ... cause, source, material and effect of all creation known, unknown, and yet to happen in the entire universe. But Brahman is not to be confused with the deity Brahma, who is a pantheistic cosmic spirit.

If you understand this, you are bound to reach Moksa and really enjoy it.

All existence—vegetable, animal, or mineral—is subject to the natural law (the eternal dharma). All good Hindus should strive to pursue ahimsa, nonviolence, and respect all forms of life—human as well as animal.

There is no single Devil, although there is a class of demons called Asuras. These imps are not evil, however; they are merely playful mischief-makers *who adore whoopee cushions, rubber chickens, and plastic doggie doo-doo.* True evil springs from human ignorance.

Hindu society has four classes: teachers and priests (Brahmanas); warriors and administrators (Kshatriyas); farmers and businessmen (Vaishyas), and servants and laborers (Shudras). Each of these classes is a Varna. The system is called Varna Vyavastha. *Say this word five times really fast for extra good karma.*

Everyone wants physical or emotional pleasure (kama), and material wealth (artha). But a good Hindu will head for the higher ground of righteousness (dharma).

Ideally, you should follow four stages of life, although this is really possible only for the Brahman class.

Spend your youth (Brahmacharya) in celibate, sober contemplation under a guru, *hopefully a thin one.*

The second stage is the Grihastya, *samsara, or the Martha Stewart-gets-married stage.* Time to have children and decorate your home.

During the third phase, Vanaprastha, you should guilt your now-grown children into supporting you. Spend your days contemplating the Divine. Go on holy pilgrimages.

Finally, in Sanyasa, after a lifetime of contemplating the Divine, go looking for Him. Start packing for your next life or, if you're really, really lucky, for liberation into the great nothing …

It's good to have at least a nodding acquaintance of the sacred texts. The four Vedas (the Rig, Yajur, Sama, and Atharva Vedas) are *shakhas* (branches) of knowledge. The overwhelming majority of Hindus never actually read these, but think highly of them nonetheless, *like English professors think of Proust.*

The Bhagavad Gita, often affectionately referred to as the Gita, is one of the more popular sacred texts of Hinduism. It is a summary of the Vedic, Yogic, Vedantic, and Tantric branches of philosophy. *"In-A-Gadda-Da-Vida" is also popular. The Iron Butterfly is a highly regarded symbol of delicate strength.*

QUALITY RATINGS:

Possible Perks: ★ ★ —You'll like this place if blue skin appeals to you, and it doesn't creep you out to worship Gods with elephant heads or multiple appendages.

Like yoga? This afterlife includes spiritual devotion (Bhakti yoga), selfless service (Karma yoga), and knowledge and meditation (Jnana or Raja yoga).

Was one of your childhood dreams to have a pet cow? Here, cows are revered, *known as the holy-cow principle.*

Hanker to decorate your home with posters of elephant-headed Gods waving myriad arms? There are many spiffy designs for decorating your home shrine. One is the Swastika, which represents truth and stability. *Although it's not too popular everywhere, and I wouldn't get one as a bumper sticker.* Also popular is the Mandala of the hexagram, which symbolizes the perfect union between the male and female. *Even more of a stretch than the holy cow.*

Relish body painting? The *tilaka* is a mark, usually applied with sandalwood paste (worn on the forehead and other places), that opens the mystic third eye and awakens supernatural consciousness.

Music: ★ ★ —Entirely monodic. Each piece is more or less based upon a single melody. *I began to imagine I was trapped in an elevator with a badly mangled George Harrison CD.*

Food: ★ ★ —Spicy. Hopefully your current reincarnation will have a strong stomach.

Drink: ★ —Milk *(very holy and good for your bones)* and ghee, a kind of clarified butter, definitely an acquired taste.

Accommodations: ★★★ —Totally dependent upon which rein-carnation you are in at the moment.

Entry Requirements: ★★ —Nothing (moksa) is difficult.

Overall Rating: ★★

Angels and Demons

If I were two-faced, would I be wearing this one?
—Abraham Lincoln

Angelica had moved in. Dirk was not sure how it had happened. At first, she would spend the night, bringing only a toothbrush and a change of clothes. Then, she cleared out a few drawers. Gradually, she annexed half the bathroom. They never discussed it, but Dirk was content. He had never lived with a woman. He didn't like the fact that she was his guardian angel, but she was smart, funny, loved sex, and made him happy.

He and Angelica were lying in bed postcoitaling, when a knock sounded at the door.

"Just a minute," Dirk called. Hastily wrapping Angelica's transparent tiger-striped, feather-trimmed robe about himself, he opened the door. Lucifer was standing on his stoop, bottle of wine in one hand, Dirk's newly submitted notes in the other.

"Nice work," Lucifer said, eyeing Dirk's striped detumescence. "I hope I'm not disturbing you. I just wanted to go over a few things." He stepped into the apartment.

"Well, actually—" Dirk began. A *hisss* sounded from behind him. Turning, he saw Angelica. Her mouth was open; her canines had grown. From her throat issued a sound Dirk had heard only in horror movies, usually occurring when the undead claim their own.

"You," she snarled in undulcet tones.

Dirk had to hand it to Lucifer; he was one cool Devil.

"So," Lucifer said smoothly, "it's the guardian angel. How is sex these days?"

"Satan!" Angelica hissed. "Fiend!"

"At your service, madam," he bowed.

Life was getting just too strange. It had been difficult enough learning that the girl he might be in love with was his guardian angel. Now she was hissing like an overly large serpent with fangs, and bore an uncanny resemblance to a barracuda with hair.

"I can see I have come at an inauspicious time. Sorry I intruded on your bit of heaven. Maybe we could schedule something later this week, Dirk?"

"Sure," Dirk shakily replied.

"Well then, give me a ring. Oh, and enjoy this"—he proffered the bottle. "With my compliments."

You had to give the Devil his due. He was certainly handling the situation better than Angelica.

"By the way," Lucifer turned at the doorway, "Does God know what you're up to?" He stepped out, closing the door softly behind him.

Inside, Angelica was still hissing. Dirk was relieved to notice that her canines appeared to be diminishing. He began to wonder if God knew what Angelica was up to. Now, however, did not appear to be a good time for further inquiry.

"Wine?" Dirk offered weakly.

"I wouldn't drink that Devil's brew if you paid me."

Dirk examined the wine curiously. Sure enough, the label depicted flames, emerging from a gleaming silver nail file. "Hmmm," Dirk muttered thoughtfully, "I'm sure I've had this brand before."

"Oh," Angelica jeered spitefully, "the Devil has a head for business."

"Do you mean he's in the wine business?"

"Wine, food … who knows? I certainly don't keep tabs on him. God always liked him best, the beautiful angel."

"Well," Dirk said, attempting to shift the conversation onto calmer ground, "perhaps if God got into the food business, communion wafers would taste less like cardboard. I mean really, the manufacturers would go right out of business if they hadn't convinced the Catholics to buy them."

"The pope's brother-in-law was a bankrupt baker." Angelica growled. "His business was miraculously resurrected by a Eucharist-body-cracker contract."

Dirk noticed with relief that Angelica's teeth had shrunk to their normal length.

"By the way, just what Heaven are you an angel for?"

"Oh," she replied, waving her hand in a vague circular motion, "I kind of freelance."

"If Lucifer was God's favorite, what does that make Christ?"

"Dead."

"I mean before—no—after that. Isn't he God's favorite now?"

"Surely you've been to enough afterlives to know that it depends on where you go."

"So, what's Christ like?"

"Sushi."

"Sushi?"

"Yes, he loves sushi, just can't get enough of it."

"No shit!" Dirk cried. "I always thought sushi was a prank on Americans, probably invented during the occupation of Japan. Charge an exorbitant amount for fish and don't even cook it. It's also cunningly calculated to make you appear crude and uncivilized. If you try to bite a piece of sushi in half, it falls apart and you look like a slob. If you pop one in your mouth whole, you appear a glutton."

"Well, if you were brought up on falafel and matzo, you might like sushi too."

Five Pillars or
Muhammad's Revenge

Martyrdom is the only way a man can become famous without ability.
—George Bernard Shaw

It was a lovely morning. Dirk was cleaning. With Angelica's arrival, his apartment had become a cheery place. She loved fresh flowers and bright fabrics. Dirk didn't always concur with the exuberance of her taste, but he'd never been particular about his surroundings. He enjoyed her happiness. After cleaning, he would run out for breakfast goodies—including chocolate, which Angelica constantly craved.

He strode over to the CD player to put in music to clean by. Beethoven or Beatles? Miles Davis or Marcy Playground? He decided on a collection of oldies that Mary had handpicked and recorded. They always filled him with sweet nostalgia.

Smiling, Dirk removed the CD and inserted it. *Shish!* It grabbed him. He was inexorably sucked toward and flattened through the thin black opening. He awoke surrounded by angry bearded men holding rocks. Opening his eyes wide in fright, the Devil's Press Pass shown brilliantly out his retinas. Instead of a stoning, Dirk was given a silk robe and escorted to one of the luxurious couches that were scattered throughout the garden, manned, or more accurately womanned, by beautiful maidens. Their eyes were as deep as onyx rivers, their hair soft, smooth, and velvety black. They positively radiated virginity.

"Ah well," Dirk sighed, "When in Rome …"

Getting into Islamic Heaven is like being admitted into university in many Asian countries. Elementary, junior high, and high school are brain-hurtingly difficult. Only a select few make it into college ... but if you get in, life is a party.

If you die fighting in the cause of God, *who seems rather vague about the causes he supports these days,* you will get seventy-two houris (or virgins with regenerating hymens) in addition to however many wives you already possess. There is some contention whether all good, pure Muslims will receive such bounty, or only martyrs.

"The penis of the Elected never softens. Erection is eternal"— Al-Suyuti (1505)

END DESTINATION:

Chances are extremely likely you'll be damned and spend all eternity in Hell.

Judgment Day is going to be exceedingly scary, even for the good. Wait in your grave for Judgment Day. If you are good, you get a windowed casket with a garden view. If you are damned, *which you probably are,* you will have a transom from Hell blowing hot air into your tomb.

The Qur'an specifies two exceptions to this general rule: "Warriors who die fighting in the cause of God" go straight to God, and "enemies of Islam" go immediately to Hell.

The Hadith (Sayings of the Prophet's Companions) say women will form the majority in Hell, because they are generally ungrateful nags who are never satisfied.

If you do get in, paradise is a fabulous terraced garden. You lie around on couches in silk robes of green and gold, spending days and nights dining, drinking, and deflowering.

The place is filled with houris. They have black eyes, white skin, "appetizing vaginas," and are perpetually amorous.

If you are a God-fearing Muslim woman, Paradise consists of an infinite closet filled with designer berkas.

There are also legions of immortal youth who serve wonderful, hangover-less wine.

ENTRY REQUIREMENTS:

It is absolutely vital to lack a sense of humor.

There is "the one God, who has no partner ... there is no other entity in the entire universe worthy of worship besides Him ... Muhammad (is the) last Prophet and Messenger ... His book is the Holy Qur'an, the only authentic revealed book in the world."

There are five main Pillars of Islam, *in addition to numerous picayune ones.*

First, declare your faith (Shahadah) by saying "There is no god but Allah; Muhammad is the Messenger of Allah." *Over and over and over again.*

The second pillar is prayer (Salah), which must be performed five times a day on a regular schedule. It's no good trying to cut it down to three long prayers, or one mammoth prayer session. It's five prayers at the right time of day, facing Mecca, or forget it. *A bad sense of direction is no excuse.* The five prayers are; dawn prayer (Fajr), immediately after noon prayer (Dhuhr), midafternoon prayer (Asr), sunset prayer (Maghrib), and early night prayer (Isha'a). Just to mix it up, on Friday is an extra noon prayer (Jumu'ah) that must be done in a mosque.

Doing prayer properly requires cleanliness: "When you prepare for prayer wash your faces and your hands to the elbows ... and (wash) your feet up to the ankles. If you are ritually impure bathe your whole body." Ritual impurity results from sex, menses, and the first forty days after childbirth. *Women are messy creatures—no wonder most of them end up in Hell.*

Also, "When any one of you eats, let him eat with his right hand … because the Satan eats with his left hand." Whoever eats with his left hand, the Satan eats with him. *Of course the Satan denies this, claiming to be ambidextrous.* The left hand should be reserved for removing dirt, cleaning oneself after going to the toilet, and blowing one's nose. "Use water, not paper or anything else, to clean yourself after defecation." *Kleenex and toilet paper are manufactured by the Satan.*

The third thing is the alms-tax (zakah). Usually 2.5% of one's capital, *not so bad, compared to the Mormon's 10%.*

Fourth, fast one month of each year, during Ramadan. It's not a really brutal fast, though. No breakfast or lunch, *but at dinner you can eat all the hummus you want.* Exempted from fasting are the old and the insane. The sick, elderly, travelers, and pregnant women, and nursing or menstruating women are also excused. But these must make up an equal number of days later. *Nursing, pregnant, or menstruating men go directly to Hell.*

Sometime during the last ten days of Ramadan—though the exact day is never known and is different each year—is the Night of Power (Laylat al-Qadr). "To spend that night in worship is equivalent to a thousand months of worship. Allah's reward for it is very great," *which is why he keeps it such a big secret.*

Fifth, make a pilgrimage (Hajj) to visit Mecca and Medina. *Do not try to replace these with London and Paris; in fact, you cannot even replace them with similar destinations such as Death Valley or Winnemucca. They won't accept it on Judgment Day.* The reward for the Hajj is Paradise.

At the culmination of the Hajj in Mecca, "Pilgrims stand together ... in a preview of the Last Judgment. They throw rocks at a stone pillar which represents Satan. It culminates in a festival ('Id al-Adha) celebrated in prayers, the sacrifice of an animal, *who finds this part of the ritual extremely disturbing* and the exchange of gifts."

Believe that Islam is the only true faith.

"Do not doubt that there is a God or that God is the ONE God."

Don't commit suicide, although martyrdom is the highest religious act possible. *I tried to clarify this, but all the Martyrs I met were too erect to chat.*

QUALITY RATINGS:
Perks: ★ ★ ★ —No clogged toilets. For women; no worries about free radicals or sun-damage, and no sun-block! For men, houris, food, drink, and sexy youths.
Music: ★ —Like wailing?
Food: ★ ★ ★ —Plentiful, fresh fruit, fowl, falafel, and flesh.
Drink: ★ ★ ★ ★ ★ —Great wine. You can drink all night without getting obnoxious or a hangover.
Accommodations: ★ ★ ★ ★ ★ —Gardens, couches, silk.
Entry Requirements: ★
OVERALL RATING: ★ ★ ★ (For men only)

Dirk returned late from the Garden of Paradise so richly described in the Qur'an. He was tipsy but not drunk. His silken robe hung off one shoulder at a jaunty angle.

Angelica was waiting on the couch. (Dirk doubted she ever slept).

"You've been hanging out with the houris, haven't you?" she snapped, her usually honeyed tones acid.

"Houris …" he slurred, staring at her with unfocused eyes. "Beautiful maidens, beautiful as pearls, eyes black as … black. That's pretty funny," he snorted. "Yeah, eyes black as black. Skin white as white," he howled with laughter, patting Angelica lustily on her behind.

"And their breasts," he continued, apparently unaware of Angelica's narrowing eyes, "like melons, pearly white, firmer than ripe peaches, nibbles—nipples—nipples …" He sputtered to a halt.

"Houris indeed! *Whouris* is more like it."

"But they're virgins," Dirk cried. "At least they were virgins," he continued with a lascivious smirk.

"Don't worry," Angelica said coldly. "They are still virgins. The sluts have regenerating hymens."

"They said angels couldn't sin," Dirk slurred, "because you have no free will."

"Don't believe everything you hear," Angelica said icily, "especially from a whouri." She sniffed sharply, obviously not enjoying the heady scents of Paradise. Angelica rose and entered the bedroom, shutting the door inhospitably behind her.

Dirk spent the night on the couch.

Funny, really. Never drink or copulate, so you can spend eternity drinking and copulating. If it's good enough for Heaven, why is it sinful on Earth?

Immoral Immortals

Tiger got to hunt, bird got to fly;
Man got to sit and wonder "why, why, why?"
Tiger got to sleep, bird got to land;
Man got to tell himself he understand.
—Kurt Vonnegut, Jr.

Notes:
Malaysian Scientists have invented a device that determines the direction
of Mecca from space, so Muslim astronauts can pray during missions.
Unfortunately, the problem of how to kneel in zero gravity has yet to be
solved.
"Jihad is never waged to force anybody to choose a particular religion."
Harming civilians is a no-no.
"Warriors who die fighting in the cause of God are ushered immediately
to God's presence,"
"Enemies of Islam are sentenced immediately to Hell upon death."
What if . . . a warrior dies fighting in the cause of God. He is trying to "per-
suade" an enemy of Islam, a civilian, to convert. What does God do then?

It was Sunday. Dirk had taken the entire weekend off. He and Angelica
lay comfortably in bed with a bottle of wine, although not the Devil's
brew. After his sufficient groveling, she appeared to have forgiven him
his houris.

"Look," Dirk began, "We need to talk. There's some stuff I want to
understand."

Angelica made her fingers into a delicate gun. "Shoot."

"I've been to a lot of Heavens and I have never seen any guardian angels."

"Of course not, silly," she said, ruffling his hair. "Many religions and cultures have guardian angels as part of their—not exactly theology—more like mythology. If you're born into one of them, you get a guardian angel assigned to you. We just sort of hang around, watch over our charges, and try to keep them from getting into too much trouble."

"Then what?"

"Then what, what?"

"I mean what happens then?"

"Then, my mortal darling, you die."

"And …?"

"You go where you go. You're seeing the options, aren't you?"

"Yes, but who decides?"

"Well, you do; generally speaking, you go where you believe you belong."

"And you?"

"We get a new assignment."

"Don't you ever die?"

"I'm an immortal being, my love. In your case, perhaps an immoral immortal," she giggled.

"Does God listen to prayers?"

"Maybe … sometimes … after all, everyone opens junk mail every now and then."

"What's with the teeth?"

"I prefer not to discuss that."

"Look, I need to know why my girlfriend, my guardian angel, seems to bear a decided resemblance to Dracula when she's upset."

"Oh well, if you must, you must, I suppose. It's part of the immortal packet. We can't blush or grow pale, because we don't have blood. We can't gasp in shock, since we don't have lungs. We aren't biological beings, but we have feelings. In fact, we're very emotional. There needs to be some way to vent. Some of us have teeth that grow; some of us vanish; some turn into frogs, cats, wolves, or bats … It explains a lot of your mythology, if you think about it."

"What about Lucifer?"

"What about him? You surely don't think Mr. Handsome would do anything as unattractive as growing teeth, do you? Oh no, not for God's pet. He just gets a very petite pair of horns—they're kind of cute, actually. When he's really upset he grows cloven hooves, but since he usually wears boots, you don't notice it.

"What all you humans, or at least you Western humans, don't appear to grasp, although it is clearly stated in your Bible, is that Satan is an angel too. The most beautiful. God's favorite. He didn't go through any big physical change when he left Heaven. God made sure of that. God always liked him best."

"So," Dirk inquired, attempting a diversion, "what's God like?"

"Busy."

"Does he know what you're up to?" Dirk persisted, although he felt on the verge of danger.

"Well, yes and no."

"What do you mean, yes and no? It seems to me it's more of a yes *or* no."

"Well," Angelica growled, "it's yes to the general, no to the specific. God doesn't tell us exactly how to do our work. He just trusts that it will be done. He's always been into free will, you know."

The Plastic Grail

Heaven, Heaven is a place,
a place where nothing, nothing ever happens.
—David Byrne

Angelica had bought a new blender. Dirk had a blender, but it was an antique. It creaked, grumbled, and complained, but it worked. Dirk was not in the habit of replacing appliances unless absolutely necessary; besides, he seldom used it. Angelica, however, had an affinity for the new and colorful.

"You've no idea how monotone most Heavens are," she complained, licking whipped cream from her fingers. "Nothing but gold and white, white and gold. Their reverence for antediluvian relics is practically ecclesiastical. As if Christ wouldn't have happily used a plastic grail if one had been available."

Angelica loved her new blender; she adored milkshakes and was fond of concocting exotic mixes of coffee, chocolate, Kahlua, marshmallow, caramel, rum, vanilla, cherries, ice-cream, whipped cream, and ginger.

With Angelica's help, Dirk's house had become a home. A rather brightly decorated home, but a home nonetheless. Batik silks and dyed feathers swung across walls in literally gravity defying arrangements.

Perhaps, Dirk mused, *she should open up a decorating business, "Angelic Creations. We defy Newton."*

Moving aside a newly hung swath of colorful fabric, Dirk dislodged a picture. It fell at his feet; Mary's twelve-year-old face stared up at him.

I thought I had lost that photo, Dirk thought, slowly picking it up. He had lost Mary too, albeit rather more permanently.

Grace and Graceless

If Jesus were alive today, the last thing he'd be is a Christian.
—Mark Twain

Dirk and Angelica sat side-by-side at the dining room table. Between them towered an enormous milkshake. Angelica stuck in two red-and-white striped straws.

"Want to see my impression of the outside of a barber shop?" Dirk asked. He twirled the straw between his fingers. "How about my impression of the inside? Well, it's pretty clean; the seats look like dentist chairs and there's hair on the floor."

"Ummm," Angelica wrapped her lips around her straw. "Want to taste my idea of heaven?" She sucked throatily.

Dirk followed suit, inhaling cold, thick, sweet liquid. "Umm, if you ever get tired of being a guardian angel, you'd make a first-class soda jerk." He licked vanilla foam from his lips.

"The trick," Angelica gurgled as soda bubbled at the corners of her mouth, "is to be generous with the ice-cream."

As Dirk sipped, his cheeks sucked together becoming one; they followed his lips down, down, down into sweet, wet darkness.

He awoke sticky with caramel and melted ice-cream. Above him towered a gaunt angel. His dour countenance was a striking contrast to his shimmering wings.

"And you are—?" the angel inquired haughtily, decidedly nonplussed to discover a milkshake-soaked human on his doorstep.

Dirk attempted an ingratiating smile, marred slightly by the chocolate sprinkle wedged between his front teeth.

The gatekeeper peered sharply into Dirk's eyes.

"Ah, yes," he sighed, grudgingly opening the gate and moving aside. "We were told to expect you." The angel disapprovingly handed Dirk a white gown, to which a pair of nacreous wings were glued.

I sure hope it's super glue.

Inside the gates stretched vistas of space and time, but no Einstein. Einstein was elsewhere, playing dice with God. Afterlives spread out before Dirk, multitudinous and various. It was the Protestant district. A huge complex, every sect divided by fortress walls.

In sixteenth-century Europe, a few idealists had decided to reform Catholicism. But revolution failed, and Protestants broke off, drifting apart like glaciers.

Although the over 33,000 Protestant denominations vary, they hold certain beliefs in common.

DIRK QUIGBY'S GUIDE
TO THE PROTESTANT AFTERLIFE

END DESTINATION:

Believers ascend to Heaven where they wait for their bodies, which will be delivered *vacuumed and detailed,* after the Second Coming. *Though beautiful, they have the sexless appearance of Ken dolls. I cannot offer a first-hand review as only the chosen get bodies.*

The damned descend to Hell, worse than an eternal root canal.

ENTRY REQUIREMENTS:

Man (especially woman) is born bad. God, in His infinite wisdom and foresight, decided a long, long time ago, possibly even before Creation, who was to be damned and who would proceed to Heaven. There is nothing you can do about this. God is the team captain and he makes the cuts.

There is only one God. God the Father, the Son, and the Holy Spirit, who are separate but equal. Why, you might inquire, if He is one, does he have three names? If you are asking questions like this, it is probably a sign you are not one of the chosen.

Baptism should only be between consenting adults, you and God.

Most Protestants, including Seventh-day Adventists and Mormons, are into total immersion baptism. *I think they didn't get to go swimming when they were kids.*

Practice foot washing. *Why if you are being totally immersed, do you have to wash your feet separately?*

You must believe that the Bible is the inspired word of God, one hundred percent true and without error. *This made me wonder if these folks have really read it—Revelations, for example, which is weird to say the least. Or the tale of Lot, who willingly gives his daughters to a crowd of marauding rapists in order to protect a couple of angels, who presumably have supernatural powers and can defend themselves.*

Attend Communion quarterly. No real wine though, so Christ's "blood" is Grape juice, or *Kool-Aid.* No transubstantiation:"wine does not lose its 'wine-ness,' but it is also actual blood."Which proves you don't need to hold services in Latin to be incomprehensible.

Accept Jesus as your personal savior. No intermediaries necessary.

Don't drink alcohol, dress in revealing clothes, wear make-up, or enjoy exotic foods. *I knew there was a reason I didn't like menudo.*

You get to hang with God. Though I didn't meet God, as he was off spying on some of the chosen.

Mennonites, Amish, and Quakers are all Anabaptists, meaning, "baptized again." *Once is never enough with a God like you.*

The Mennonite Church has been in existence for more than 475 years. *They are extremely proud of this, even though pride is a major sin, and I have visited a host of older Heavens.*

In 1525, a small group of believers began declaring their faith in Jesus Christ and re-baptizing each other publicly. The Catholic Church thought this extremely gauche. To curtail this embarrassing behavior, the Church persecuted, and whenever time permitted, martyred them.

During these halcyon early days of mayhem and murder, there lived in the Netherlands a priest named Menno Simons. He was rethinking his Catholic faith. For one thing, he was having difficulty believing in transubstantiation. *He uncorked the wine, poured it into the chalice, but never, never saw it turn to blood. His bishop said that a watched chalice never transubstantiates, but he doubted.*

Shortly after Menno's fortieth birthday, his brother was killed by Catholic soldiers. *Happy Birthday, Menno!*

Into a nearby confessional booth ... out comes Super-Mennonite, founder of the church, which bears his name.

END DESTINATION:

Heaven or Hell. And if you have indulged in such sins as eating McDonald's fries, Fat Burgers, or listening to Madonna *(the singer, not the virgin)*, you will be sentenced to everlasting torment in Hell. *God hates trans-fat and pop music.* As for Heaven, see "Perks."

ENTRY REQUIREMENTS:

First God created the world. Humanity really messed up in the Garden of Eden, but Jesus saves. God exists, and don't you doubt it.

Speaking in tongues is recognized *but not understood.*

As in most places, women ministers not allowed.

Never swear oaths on the Bible in judicial proceedings. This is against the teachings of Jesus; however, you can make solemn affirmations. *Such as, "Love your bonnet," or, "Well, confiscate my buggy!"*

Spy on your neighbors. If you notice anything sinful, e.g. *a Big Mac wrapper or a Rolling Stones CD,* warn the offenders twice privately. Then, publicly condemn and ban them.

If the pastor is led to martyrdom, get another within the hour.

No military service; some choose not to pay the percentage of income tax that supports the military. *Warning: if you are not a Mennonite, this is known as "tax evasion."*

Accept that this is the only true church of Jesus Christ.

QUALITY RATINGS FOR MENNONITE HEAVEN:

Perks: ★ —Homemade food, homemade furniture, homemade quilts.

Music: ★ —Musical instruments are worldly. Sing a cappella. Enjoy the Altar of Praise Chorale and the Smucker Family singers. *With names like that, they have to be good!*

The Mennonites have many hymns but few melodies. It was more than a tad monotonous even for a visit, let alone eternity.

Drink: ★ —Milk

Food: ★★★ —Chicken, ham, mashed potatoes, gravy, relishes, and canned fruit, plus cookies, cakes, and pies. *Is Heavenly cholesterol "good" cholesterol or "bad" cholesterol?*

Accommodations: ★★ —Simple and clean. The land is divided into neat squares of well tended farms. In the distance I saw what I assumed to be a crop burning gone wild, but I was wrong. On a clear day you can't see forever, but you can see hell, where all non-Mennonites sizzle.

Entry Requirements: ★

OVERALL RATING: ★★

PRESBYTERIANISM (AKA CALVINISM)

Based on the teaching of John Calvin, not a man noted for his frolicsome spirit. This is the only true church of Jesus Christ.

QUALITY RATINGS FOR PRESBYTERIAN HEAVEN:

Perks: ★★★ —Enjoy annoying others with how pious you are.

Music: ★ —Organs, vocals, and really monotonous tunes.

Food: ★★ —Meat and potatoes. Food and drink here are very plain. After a lifetime of being good, the pure and dutiful evidently haven't developed epicurean tastes.

Drink: ★ —Milk, juice, and water (see Food).

Accommodations: ★★ —Clean, golden, and spare. Heaven is surrounded by a wall of clear fire. Here all non-Calvinists suffer eternal torment, and you can watch!

Entry Requirements: ★

OVERALL RATING: ★★

THE BAPTISTS

To enjoy the fruits of this afterlife, you must renounce any "habits" that are enjoyable. Why? Because, although Heaven will be (literally) paved with gold, mansions, and loved ones, it will require adjustment. If you have too much fun on Earth, Heaven will seem boring. *Not much of a recommendation.*

You must believe this is the only true church of Jesus Christ.

Although in this afterlife we retain our sexual identity, there is no sex. Your new, improved body is perpetually fixed at either twenty-one, because that's a good age, or thirty-three, because that's when Jesus was crucified. In the words of one of their wretched songs—"I Wanna be Just Like Geeee-zuz." Blue balls are not my idea of paradise!

QUALITY RATINGS FOR BAPTIST HEAVEN:

Perks: ★ —The main selling point is possibly getting to skip death. If you are really, really good—no dancing (too much like sex), no sex (too much like dancing), no drinking, gambling, or gamboling, then you do not stop for death but proceed directly to Heaven. This is translation, because you are translated directly from a boring life into a boring Heaven, without pausing along the way to decompose.

Music: ★ —Earplugs a must. Music is piped in and professional singers are far too worldly for this afterlife. The only relief is near the fence of surrounding fire. If the wind blows right, the shrieks of the damned drown out the ubiquitous music.

Food: ★ —Greasiness is Next to Godliness. Deep Fried Twinkies are popular. They can be fried in vegetable oil, beef suet, or tallow, and topped with powdered sugar and caramel, chocolate, or raspberry dipping sauce.

Drink: ★ —Only secretly.

Accommodations: ★ ★ —Mansions with Astroturf.

Entry Requirements: ★

OVERALL RATING: ★

ASSEMBLIES OF GOD/PENTECOSTALISTS

END DESTINATION:

The streets are paved with gold, but up here, perhaps due to a lack of atmosphere, gold looks like glass.

There is no sun because Christ freelances as the Light, the Son/Sun.

ENTRY REQUIREMENTS:

Be a baptized believer.

Speaking in tongues (known as glossolalia, *or gibberish*) is a sign that you have the Holy Spirit inside, and He wants out. After all, He's used to space and golden glass streets. Now, He's stuck inside your esophagus. *No wonder He's so vociferous.* If you do not speak in tongues you are probably damned and going to Hell.

Snake-handling is practiced among a minority of Pentecostals. They fondle poisonous snakes (usually copperheads or rattlers), play with fire, and drink water laced with strychnine, arsenic, or available cleaning products. If you are bitten, poisoned, or burned, it is because you lack faith. Not only may you die, but if you do, you will go to Hell.

Believe that this is the only true church of Jesus Christ.

God, in His infinite wisdom, doesn't consign babies or those too stupid to understand the requirements of faith to eternal fire. Babies and brainless people proceed directly to Heaven. *The place was swarming with them! At least I think it was ... I had some difficulty distinguishing the idiots. I had no trouble identifying the babies though; they were smaller and smelled better.*

I did not try on one of the remodeled bodies, due to a fear of snakes.

**QUALITY RATINGS FOR ASSEMBLIES OF GOD/
PENTECOSTAL HEAVEN:**

Perks: ★★ —If you want to speak a foreign language, this is the place for you. Speaking in tongues is an act of holiness and no one can correct your grammar or pronunciation.

Music: ★ —Boisterous, fervent and out of tune.

Food: ★ —Substance is different, it lacked spice.

Drink: ★ —Grape juice.

Accommodations: ★★★ —Horribly bright. Not only is there the Son/Sun and the glass, but heaven is surrounded by a scorching inferno and the smell of burning flesh. An angel informed me it was the nonbelieving Baptists burning. As least I think that's what he said, they speak glossolalia here. Sunglasses recommended.

Entry Requirements: ★

OVERALL RATING: ★

That night Dirk's dreams were haunted by angels with beautiful, disapproving faces.

Timeless Stories on TV

*It is a lot better to come from an evolved monkey
than from a fallen angel.* —Marcellin Boule

Dirk and Lucifer met at a small outdoor café to discuss the upcoming release of *Dirk Quigby's Guide to the Afterlife*.

"I had a nice childhood," Lucifer began nibbling his salade nicoise. "Not childhood exactly—creation; that's it, a good creation. I got along well with most of the angels, all except Michael, Peter, and Gabriel. Talk about stuffed wings!" He sipped his Pinot Grigio.

"I was an artistic angel. I liked to draw, design worlds, that sort of thing. It's a little-known fact, but I designed the seahorse!" Lucifer modestly gazed down at his salad.

"Then God sponsored a contest: design the future! I entered, of course. I thought it would be nice if people loved each other and got along. I thought that no wars, hatred, or pollution would be a good thing, but noooo … I made the mistake of wanting a little credit. Even assistant gaffers get their names on screen.

"Working for God is like drawing for Disney. You do the work; he gets the residuals.

"Michael, on the other hand, wanted a lot of illness, pain, and hate. He called it 'free will.' Of course he didn't want credit for that! Well, that's when all hell broke loose (if you'll pardon the expression). So, here I am, just trying to reduce my workload …

"We'll start with a small first edition, only ten afterlives, sort of a 'teaser.'"

"I think we should leave out the Baptists," said Dirk, who still had the Baptist heaven "Golden Bells for You and Me" running though his head. "That will only appeal to people who have really pathetic taste in music."

"Let's get the show on the road. The first edition comes out in a month; you need to be on talk shows NOW!" he said slapping the table. "You're booked on *Michael Guy Alright* Sunday."

"Michael Guy Alright! Why, that's the biggest show on TV! How'd you manage that?"

The Devil spread his carefully manicured fingers, "I'm the Devil. I have connections. Fiends are very heavy into the industry. Don't you watch TV? You don't think that's God's work, do you?"

Quake, Rattle 'n' Roll

Some look at things that are, and ask why. I dream of things that never were and ask why not? —George Bernard Shaw

Wednesday—Supposed to visit the Shinto afterlife, but this belief has no division between the hereafter and the here, the spirit or the corporeal. How in hell am I supposed to visit?

Dirk jogged to the corner store. Angelica needed chocolate. He needed coffee and cigarettes. Ahead of him hobbled an ancient man, using a three-legged cane.

Dirk sighed. He thought of his once-beautiful mother. She too was now old. She too now needed a cane, although she refused to use one.

His memory took him back to his last visit to Lulu. She in the hospital, recovering from a fall, as well as receiving her bi-monthly blood infusion, required as her own blood contained near-toxic levels of alcohol. "A cane makes me look old and feeble," she snapped. Dirk barely refrained from retorting, "But you are old and feeble."

Ahead of Dirk, the old man slipped, tottered, and fell. Dirk bent over. The man grabbed his arm. Dirk was surprised by the strength of his grasp. Dirk levered his weight, trying to right him. The old man pulled back. Dirk felt a by-now familiar, but nevertheless sickening, sensation. He wriggled and writhed as he was wrenched down, down into blackness.

A plain white fence bordered this Heaven. Inset into the fence was an oval portrait of a smiling gentleman with shoulder-length white hair, a black suit, broad-brimmed hat, and white cravat. He seemed familiar. WELCOME FRIENDS was embossed on the gate in hammered brass letters.

Founded by George Fox, circa 1645, Quakers (so called because they "tremble in awe before the Lord") are known as "the Society of Friends."

END DESTINATION:

Quakerism is concerned with this world and has no theology of Heaven or Hell.

Although Quakerism has deep Christian roots, not all Quakers consider themselves Christian. *As a result, there is a fair amount of confusion.* Some Quakers believe you will go to Hell if you do not follow God's spirit within you, but most don't believe it will last for eternity. Others claim there is no Hell, and a great many don't believe in an afterlife. *Those Friends stayed in their graves.*

Many believe that Heaven will be a "peaceable kingdom," like Earth, only better. *I find the notion that Earth is in any way, shape or form a peaceable kingdom endearing yet wacky.*

Upon arrival, you might be given a new body, mind, and spirit, or not.

If there is an afterlife, you will recognize loved ones: "Both spiritual and corporeal intercourse are celebrated here."

If you want to co-author a book or mate with an alien, this might be the Heaven for you. "Fifty billion galaxies ... offer venue for creative thought and activity."

The Quaker afterlife can vary from fundamentalist Christian to atheistic. However, if you follow the striving of God within you, you will (probably) not die.

ENTRY REQUIREMENTS:

Christ may or may not be God or the son of God. But, as a spirit, He is universally available, and has been so since the beginning of Creation. Our job is to listen to our inner Christ. Christ is actually present during personal and group worship.

Friends affirm "experiential," not "virtual" reality. *Not a good destination for computer nerds.*

Quakers do not believe in state-financed ministries or loyalty oaths. *Both Herbert Hoover and Richard Nixon were raised as Quakers.*

Quakerism has no formal creed. *They can't even agree on whether or not God exists, or if they're Christians. How in heaven can they concoct a creed?*

Holiness exists in everything.

Divine revelation is available to all.

Physical baptism is bosh.

Any shared meal is a communion, *even 99-cent burritos eaten with your left hand.*

Early Quakers wore plain clothes to combat vanity, conformity, and waste. This practice has been discontinued because Quakers were becoming vain about their plainness. *The inception of the Ms. Plain Universe contest was a decided blow to many believers.*

Plainness in speech promotes honesty and erases class distinctions.

Never swear an oath, not even in court *or if you drop a hammer on your foot.* The act of swearing to tell the truth implies that this is not something you normally do. Honesty is more than not telling lies. You must not mislead others. *A very bad place for politicians, attorneys, salespeople, and spouses.*

Avoid bargaining for goods. *Don't shop in Mexico or Mecca.*

Don't use honorific titles.

A few Friends retain use of "thou" and "thee" with other Friends, *but if thee is not comfortable with thou, it's okay.*

Don't use more than your fair share of Earth's resources, *about a goat and a half, plus five eggs, a basket of zucchini, and one chocolate bar.*

Everyone is equal. Women and men have always had the same authority. Friends campaigned for women's rights, were leaders in the anti-slavery movement, and pioneered for humane treatment of prisoners and the mentally ill. *You have to admire these folks. On the other hand, how fully can one admire a religion whose greatest visual achievement is to display their founder's face on a round tin of breakfast cereal?*

There are two styles of service. In an unprogrammed service, Friends gather in silence. When a member wants to share, he or she rises and gives "ministry."

Programmed worship was introduced to make converts comfortable. It includes readings from scripture, hymns, and a sermon, as well as the sound of silence.

To get married, simply declare your intention at a meeting. No one conducts the ceremony. Couples marry each other before God and the witnesses. Same-sex marriages are also celebrated.

Business meetings are a form of worship. *By this I don't mean that the universal incantation, "I pray this meeting will be over soon," is silently invoked.* There is no voting. A decision is reached when the meeting feels that God's will for the community has been made clear.

Violence is wrong.

Everything is a form of worship. God is the center of life.

QUALITY RATINGS:
Perks: ★ ★ ★ —You obtain a circle of Friends.

Music: ★ —None. Singing, the repetition of written verses, is not inspired by God's spirit. *Especially some of the hymns I've been subjected to lately.*

Food: ★★ —Like oatmeal?

Drink: ★★ —Like apple juice?

Accommodations: ★★★ —Clean and simple

Entry Requirements: ★★★★

OVERALL RATING: ★★★★

Raw Deals

In theory, there is no difference between theory and practice.
But, in practice, there is. —Jan L.A. van de Snepscheut

Angelica and Dirk were out to dinner. The restaurant was on the second floor of a modern green-glass and steel mall.

They were carried to the restaurant by a gleaming escalator that scaled an unnaturally blue pond in which glistened pennies and carp. The carp occasionally leapt from the water; the pennies sat on the bottom looking bored.

The restaurant specialized in raw cuisine, which was much more expensive than cooked food.

"I don't get it," Dirk said. "The less work that goes into preparing a meal, the more it costs."

"Kind of an existential dining experience," Angelica agreed, munching on some uncooked brown rice. "This must be really good for your teeth."

"I sure hope it's good for something," Dirk replied, "because it tastes beastly."

After a pricy dessert of sugar cane and unprocessed, intensely bitter, cacao beans. They were presented a two-volume check. Volume I: minuscule, unidentifiable appetizers—through tiny, tough entrées. Volume II: chewy, winey, grapes—through dangerously acidic coffee.

"This," Dirk said, "is what I call a raw deal."

"At least we didn't get the unroasted espresso or the unfermented Chateau la fete."

Leaving the restaurant, they mounted the descending escalator. Its revolving teeth snatched Dirk's trouser. Reaching down, he tried to extract his pants without doing irreparable damage to the fabric. Slowly and painfully, the teeth began to munch his hand. He shrieked, screamed, and thrust his body upward in frantic effort, but it was no use. He was inexorably being masticated into another world. Mercifully, he lost consciousness.

He came to, his shirt mangled and his trousers shredded, in front of a plain wooden fence of immense proportions.

DIRK QUIGBY'S GUIDE TO THE AMISH AFTERLIFE

In 1693, Jacob Amman, a Mennonite leader, felt the Church was getting too worldly. For instance, though Mennonites practiced Meidung (shunning), it was a piddling, half-assed Meidung. Families had been known to eat together even when one was being shunned. Now, what kind of Meidung is that?

In addition, the Mennonites were just not doing enough foot washing. *There was even a documented case of bromidrosis (stink-foot) among the congregation.* Amman demanded more foot washing and Meidunging. The Mennonites resisted. Amman excommunicated them. Later he thought better of it and recommunicated them. But it was too late—the Mennonites split, citing *irreconcilable differences. Thus, from the milk of human kindness, brotherly love, and tolerance were the Amish born.*

END DESTINATION:

Heaven or Hell. Salvation is by the grace of God, *who can withhold it if he's in a bad mood.* You can never be certain where you are going until you die, and God hands the envelope to St. Peter.

There are no cameras in Heaven because taking a picture is like making a "graven image," and is extremely naughty. For this reason, dolls have no faces, *which I found decidedly creepy.*

Shun electricity, automobiles, and buttons. *Learn Pennsylvania Dutch, a dialect of German that nobody speaks, or be voiceless. Being voiceless wouldn't be bad, as it would prevent declarations of personal preference.*

Follow the Mennonite doctrine plus some.

Amish men have beards because *those Bible guys were hairy dudes. Mustaches, on the other hand, have a long history of residing on the upper lips of military men and are therefore forbidden.*

Use hooks and eyes instead of buttons on your outer garments, because it is a well-known fact that military gents are very fond of buttons. Such ornamentation might make you feel violent or proud. *You can sew buttons on your underwear, though.*

One's clothing should be plain and not draw attention to the wearer. *If you have camouflage, don it.*

Have horror of Hochmut (pride) and value Demut and Gelassenheit (submission to God).

Buggies must have wire wheels. *I'm not sure why rubber is sinful, but it is.*

There are the "black-bumper Amish" who have decided that cars are fine as long as they are chrome-less. Best shun them.

The Bible tells us not to "conform to the world," so be a non-conformist! You had better conform to the Amish rules however, or it's Meidung city. "Ordnung" is the oral tradition of rules, which regulate everything. It's absorbed by osmosis during your youth.

From first- to eighth-grade you *are taught English and obsolete German, in a one-room schoolhouse. After that, quit school—from what I remember of high school, a definite plus. The teachers are Amish and have no more than an eighth-grade education. Post-eighth grade, you are unlikely to learn anything useful, like how to milk a cow, raise a barn, or sew hooks and eyes on clothing. The road to Hell is paved with PhDs.*

Leaving school isn't all skittles and grits, however; you will work hard and be grateful. Child labor laws often attempt to interfere with God's laws.

Children must follow the will of their parents in all things. However, in adolescence, you can experiment ("Rumspringa and herumspringen," or, running and jumping around). After that, make a permanent commitment to the Church and get baptized. Otherwise—meidung. Some communities actively shun those who leave, even if it's just to join the Amish congregation down the street. You must not buy from, sell to, or eat with a nonbeliever even if they are your spouse, sibling, or offspring. *It's God's plan, though it makes family gatherings a tad tense.* Other communities keep close family and social ties even with those who leave the Church and shun shunning. *They are going to Hell.* Remember, this is the only true church of Jesus Christ.

Communities are constantly breaking up over how many buttons should be allowed, how to meidung, and when to meidung.

There is hot contention between "one-suspender" and "two-suspender" groups and schisms over how many pleats should be on a bonnet.

Groups with similar policies can intermarry, which is necessary to avoid becoming the "Amish of West Virginia" rather than the "Amish of Lancaster."

You will need to pay most, but not all, taxes.

Quality Ratings:
Perks: ★ ★ ★ —You will not have to pay Social Security; but, you won't collect either. *Still, the way things are going …*

No military service.

You won't have to change to compact fluorescents,
No anxiety about the latest fashions, or razor bumps.
No SATs.

Music: ★ —Songs are in German, using ancient singing styles not found elsewhere, because they are monophonic, monotonous, unvarying, and boring. They stalwartly lack meter or harmony, featuring long drawn-out tones. Instruments cannot be played in public *although if you can fit an organ in your closet, go right ahead.* Some songs take over fifteen minutes to sing *and at least thirty minutes to hear.* "Sings" or "Singings" are held in barns on Sunday evenings after church. They are a hang-out for courting couples, *the Amish equivalent of a drive-in.*

Food: ★ ★ ★ —*Filling, fattening, homemade, and organic.*

Drink: ★ —Milk.

Accommodations: ★ ★ ★ —Nice, clean, and rustic in style. Beautiful handcrafted furniture and handmade quilts. Drawbacks: surrounded by flames, which sometimes makes the air a bit smoky.

Entry Requirements: ★

OVERALL RATING: ★ ★

"Where have you been?" Angelica walked into the room, calmly munching a large piece of chocolate cake smothered in coffee ice-cream.

"Visiting the Amish," Dirk replied. He sighed as he considered what he had learned.

"So often, things start out well; then they get perverted. In the beginning, simplicity, humbleness, and plainness; then plainness becomes a vanity, humbleness a point of pride, and simplicity gets complicated by too many rules. Live simply, not so others can live simply, but so that you can scorn others who live less simply."

Dirk sighed again. Although he liked quilts, he hated Meidung.

Televangelism

As the poet said, "Only God can make a tree"—probably because it's so hard to figure out how to get the bark on. —Woody Allen

Dirk sat, stiff and nervous, backstage in a bright, stifling dressing room, having orange foundation applied to his face by a *zaftig* redhead. She dabbed on the makeup with the thick, sure strokes of a plasterer. Her overripe cleavage, oozing a heady mixture of synthetic flowers and sweat, hovered frighteningly under his nose.

"Don't worry," she barked, agitating a pack of Chiclets with the relentlessness of a washer on spin. "It'll look normal on stage."

Dirk stared at the unnatural orange version of himself and doubted.

"Close your eyes," she snapped, brandishing a large brush.

Before Dirk could comply, he found himself coughing under a dense cloud of fine white powder.

★

Dirk, greasy and nervous, was escorted to a battered pink room, to await entry. The walls were the color of crushed rose petals, but for some reason it was called the green room.

Dirk watched the small blurry monitor. The screen was filled with the substantial face of Michael Guy Alright. Michael Guy Alright had white-blond hair and indifferent blue eyes.

"One minute to air time."

Dirk followed the voice into the wings. He waited behind a flat palm, which gave lie to the poem, "Only God can make a tree." He gazed at the turquoise blue sea, which shimmered under the hot, white light of an interior sun.

"And now … Dirk Quigby, author of the soon to be released *Dirk Quigby's Guide to the Afterlife.*"

The small studio audience banged their hands together, their efforts enhanced by the taped clapping exploding from all corners of the studio.

"You're on."

Dirk staggered forward, blinded by the light. He stood for a moment, staring unseeing at the studio audience who welcomed him so warmly.

They had never heard of Dirk, but were responding with Pavlovian alacrity to the flashing applause signs.

Dirk wavered. Michael Guy Alright gestured toward an empty chair, and Dirk stumbled into a seat opposite his host.

"Dirk," Michael Guy Alright said in the soothing tones reserved for idiots, invalids, infants, and audiences, "you claim to have visited the 'borne from which no traveler returns' not just once but many times."

"Y-y-yes," Dirk stammered nervously. He could write good copy in his sleep, but this business of lights and live listeners made him fidgety. "I have been to Heaven … well, not just Heaven, many Heavens."

Michael Guy Alright frowned slightly, "Many Heavens? Surely there is just one."

"Well, no," Dirk said, gaining confidence slightly. "After all, you couldn't expect a Buddhist to be happy in a Pentecostal heaven, now could you? Or a Calvinist to be happy in … well, anywhere really."

"Humm," Michael Guy, sagely stroked his chin.

"I find," Dirk continued, gaining assurance with each new assertion, "that Heaven is pretty much what you make it. If you expect golden streets, the streets will shine; if you expect raw grain, you shall have it in abundance."

"Raw grain?" Michael Guy cocked a quizzical look at the camera.

"Yeah, raw grain," Dirk sighed. "For some reason the Jains are very fond of it … If they are fond of anything. I had a lot of it when I was there."

"But surely," Michael Guy said as he surreptitiously fingered the small gold cross that hung about his neck, "there is but one true way."

"Everyone seems to think so. Most folks are certain that their Heaven is the only place to be. But from what I can tell, God isn't nearly so dogmatic or judgmental."

Michael Guy smiled frostily and cut to a commercial.

Do the Right Thing

Not all those who wander are lost.
—J.R.R. Tolkien

After the show was over, the Devil took Dirk out for a celebratory drink. They sat side-by-side on red-wine leather bar stools in the dark wooden interior of an elegant old saloon.

"I don't think they liked me," Dirk said as Lucifer clinked his glass of rich burgundy against Dirk's beer.

"'Liked you,'" Lucifer repeated. "*Like* is a word that should be reserved for children and small furry animals that don't bite. 'Like' is not the emotion raised by a sojourner of afterlives. *Respect.* Now that's a word." Once again, Lucifer raised his glass to Dirk.

"It's interesting," Dirk said. "A lot of people seem more concerned about whether or not you drink coffee than whether or not you help your brother."

"Ahh," Satan, spread his magnificent fingers out in a fan, "I could be wrong, but choosing a religion or a belief has always seemed to me a bit like buying a car. People want daily affirmation. They need to be told they have made the right choice, done the right thing.

"You want to read in *Car Digest* or *Auto Weekly* that your car is THE AUTOMOBILE OF THE CENTURY, that it's the acme of autos, the superlative sedan, the climax of cars, the unbeatable vehicle. You want people to say, 'Hey, great car, you made a great buy!'

"Well, religion is kind of the same. Most people require a daily affirmation. It's easier to obtain that by following a strict set of guidelines than by trying to address the amorphous question of 'goodness.'

"At the end of the day, you can proclaim, 'I have tithed' or 'I have not drunk coffee or wine today, therefore I must be good and am on my way to Heaven.' It's a lot more difficult and demanding to truly help another person, or to consecrate one's life to follow the just and righteous path. It's also much harder to delineate. It's easier to not drink wine, even to refrain from sex, than to be completely certain of doing 'the right thing,' let alone doing it! But that's where you come in, buddy; you can provide the undecided with guidance, entry requirements, and assurances. You are the '*Auto Weekly* for Heaven'!"

Dirk smiled weakly. He was not altogether certain he desired to be the Auto Weekly for Heaven.

Golden Questions

In heaven, all the interesting people are missing.
—Friedrich Nietzsche

Dirk was returning home from the library. He had decided to share with Angelica the favorite stories of his youth. His car contained *Charlotte's Web*, *Stuart Little*, and *Tales from the Arabian Nights*. They would read aloud to each other. Dirk smiled happily, imagining Angelica listening to these tales of magic and wonder. Then she would read to him and like the sultan entranced by Scheherazade, he would succumb to the deep, rich velvet of her voice.

Dirk pulled into a yellow zone and sprinted out of his car toward an ATM machine. He inserted his bankcard. Before he could remove his hand, scream, or even consider screaming, he was sucked hungrily into the slot. Dirk was flattened to the width of a credit card and slurped into blackness.

He awoke in front of a gate so clean it hurt his eyes. FAMILIES WELCOME was neatly hand-lettered over the entrance, to the heaven of the Church of Jesus Christ of the Latter-Day Saints.

DIRK QUIGBY'S GUIDE TO THE MORMON AFTERLIFE

In 1820, fourteen-year-old Joseph Smith, Jr. had a problem: which religion was the righteous one? He went into the woods and prayed for guidance. Jesus and his dad showed up, giving Joe some amazing news:

Every church on Earth was offensive to the Lord.

Joseph was instructed to found a new religion; it would be the one true Church of Jesus Christ. A spiritual guide would tell him what to do.

Joe waited for months, but no one appeared. A year later, no one continued appearing.

Finally, after three years, an angel named Moroni showed up with some gold tablets.

Moroni gave Joe a couple of rocks to put in his eyes so that he could translate the tablets from "Reformed Egyptian" into the *Book of Mormon: Another Testament of Jesus Christ.* The rocks, or "seer stones," were named the Urim and Thummim, *Urmie and Thumie to their friends.* Joseph put the rocks over his eyes and covered his face with his hat, shutting out all earthly distraction *and looking damn silly.* When Joseph had compiled the Book of Mormon, Moroni returned and repossessed the gold plates, *which is why they aren't on exhibit next to the Ten Commandments, the Ark of the Covenant, the genuine Shroud of Turin, and the Holy Grail in the Lost Artifacts of God Museum.*

In the 1840's, God stopped by for a chat with Joe and told him that having multiple wives was super righteous. Boy, was his wife pissed!

Although extremely charismatic, Joseph was not universally popular. He collected a group of followers, but after being tarred, feathered, and violently expelled from Ohio and Missouri, Joseph Smith was killed trying to escape from prison in Illinois.

Brigham Young was proclaimed the group's new prophet and revelator. He led the faithful, including multiple wives, to the land of milk, honey, and salt, in Zion, aka Salt Lake City. Salt Lake City, the only place in the world where even the Jews are Gentiles. Mormons call everyone who isn't a Mormon "a Gentile." *Go figure.*

In 1890, God told Church President Wilford Woodruff that he

(God), after some consideration, had decided that maybe plural marriages weren't a good idea. In fact, they were wrong and forbidden! *The fact that the United States Army was about to invade Utah had absolutely nothing whatsoever to do with God's decision.*

Mormonism is the fastest growing religion in the world. *Although not as fast as in their days of polygamy.* Of course, it helps to have over sixty thousand dazed twenty-year-olds, wandering the world on two-year missions and baptizing new recruits. Vicarious Baptism for the Dead (performed in Mormon temples) helps swell the membership ranks, if not with lay Mormons, at least with laid-to-rest Mormons. *I love baptizing the dead; they never struggle when you hold them under.*

END DESTINATION:

Three levels of heavenly tiers: the Celestial Kingdom, the Terrestrial Kingdom, and the Telestial Kingdom. The male overachievers in the Celestial Kingdom can go on to become Gods. The afterlife is a series of steps leading to Godhood.

The outer darkness is a holding tank for the souls of the wicked. Here they remain until the end of the millennium, when they will be resurrected and judged. Most will be allowed to limbo into the Telestial Kingdom. Murders, apostates, sons of perdition, and *Sunday Golfers* will return to outer darkness—this time for eternity.

ENTRY REQUIREMENTS:

In the pre-existence, we were all angels. During the great God/Satan Debates *of 00 BC (Before Creation)*, one-third of the 144,000 angels sided with Satan. Satan's team lost the fracas *along with their apartments* and were damned to Hell forever, so we can forget about them. The rest backed up God, but some, instead of valiantly fighting, *ran away and cowered behind clouds.* "Those who were less valiant in the pre-existence are known to us as the Negroes."

The Church has reformed this ideology, however, and now states: *"Those who were less valiant in the preexistence are known to us as the African-Americans."* Until 1978, black males were denied the priesthood. Black females as well as all females are still denied the priesthood, as well as Godhood. "Dark skin is a curse from God and a sign of his displeasure." *Vaginas are apparently not too great either.*

However, if you are a really good brown person, God (in generations) will wash away the curse and you will turn white!

In 1978, God revealed that blacks were finally ready to be ordained. *The fact that Brigham Young University couldn't get anyone to play sports with them had absolutely nothing to do with it.*

The Book of Mormon focuses on a tribe of Jews who sailed from Jerusalem to the New World in 600 BC. (*Leif Erickson and Columbus can go suck eggs*).

Around that time there lived in Jerusalem a super-righteous Jew named Lehi. None of the other Jews liked Lehi, because he kept showing up at parties and prophesying the impending destruction of Jerusalem. Finally, Lehi and his sons, Laman, Lemuel, Nephi, and Sam, left Jerusalem to sail to America, presumably *by the way of the Dead Sea.* Before departing for the New World, Lehi sent his sons back to Jerusalem to pick up some wives and sacred brass plates containing their genealogy and history.

Laban, possessor of the brass plates, didn't want to give them up. Laman, Lemuel and Sam tried to beg, buy, and steal them, but nothing worked. Finally, Nephi got them the old-fashioned, righteous way. He cut Laban's head off, and stole the brass plates along with Laban's servant.

Thus, the Jews, under the moral guidance of Nephi and his shanghaied servant, sailed to America. Once on land, the Jews split into two warring factions. The God-fearing Nephites were "white and delightsome," while the idol-worshiping Lamanites were "dark and loathsome." The dark, filthy, and loathsome Lamanites are "the principal ancestors of the American Indians, Polynesians, and New World Latinos." Thus it is that Native Americans, Polynesians, and New World Latinos are really the descendents of one of the lost tribes of Israel. *Funny, they don't look Jewish.*

By AD 385, the dark-skinned Lamanites had wiped out the other Hebrews. However, the good news is that if the Lamanites return to the Church, their skin will once again become white. *I have been monitoring the Mormon Church's spread throughout Mexico but have yet to notice any pigment changes.*

The Book of Mormon is the divine, unchanging, and unchangeable word of God, yet oddly enough, it keeps altering. For instance, in 1981, the Nephites transformed from a "white and delightsome people" into a "pure and delightsome people." *But hold the Book of Mormon up to a mirror and you can still make out the truth.*

After his crucifixion, Christ took the scenic route to Heaven, stopping off to visit the New World and spending time in such hot spots as Panama, Honduras, and Ohio. While vacationing in the Americas, Christ picked up twelve new disciples. Before leaving for Heaven, he granted each disciple one wish.

Nine asked to live long healthy lives serving Christ, and then to hang with him in Heaven. The remaining three decided to tarry on earth a little—like till the end of it. They desired everlasting life so they could continue to wander the globe proselytizing. There are numerous sightings of the three Nephites. There's scarcely a locale in Utah that has not been visited by the Three Nephites with their bone white feet, their flowing white hair, their long white beards, and their white, delightsome, teeth. *They are good friends of Elvis and Jimmie Dean. If you see a Nephite, please alert your nearest Nephite representative.*

I met the six dead disciples. They were having a Jell-O cook off and studying to be Gods.

★

God was a man who progressed to Godhood. If you study hard, you too can be a God.

If you are a woman, you need to obey your husband. *After all he's going to be God.*

Tithe ten percent of your income to the Church, otherwise you are not allowed inside the temple. Only members who have anteed up and have temple recommendations can participate in the secret rites.

Follow the "Word of Wisdom" and shun alcohol, smoking, caffeine, and fornication. Mormons take the "no sex without marriage" commitment very seriously, even though it's a much more limited proposition in today's monogamous society. *However, dry humping is very popular.*

Be prepared. Keep a two-year supply of food and drink at home in case God comes down and closes all the supermarkets. *Most of the homes I visited seem to have continued this custom in heaven, although I have no idea why. Here, the refrigerators never need defrosting and the storage is heavenly!*

Quality Ratings:

Possible Perks: ★ ★ —Mormons keep progressing in the afterlife and eventually become gods themselves.

Even if you are dead and wasting away in hell, you can still get into this afterlife if baptized vicariously by a living Mormon.

In Heaven, you will be forever bonded with your family, *a dubious delight.*

Men can be sealed to multiple wives but not the reverse. *Warning: this sometime leads to a bit of trouble in Paradise.*

Women spend eternity cleaning.

Men who go for Masonic-type rituals will love this place. Boys enter the Aaronic priesthood as early as age twelve. When you're eighteen you can get the Melchizedek priesthood and *a decoder ring!*

In the Temple, if you've paid up, you get to wear neat costumes and participate in arcane rituals. Many of the rites involve wearing shower caps and green aprons in the shape of a fig leaf.

You get to "play dead." You enter a dark room where chosen members of the faith pretend to be spirits. *This is presumably to prepare you for the afterlife, although it's hard to take it too seriously if "God" sounds like your Uncle Jo Bob or your sixth-grade mathematics teacher.*

Everyone's taught a secret handshake and gets a secret name so that God will know you belong in Heaven. (Women can tell men their secret names but not visa-versa.)

Both sexes get special underwear. *This may appeal to those who missed out on summer camp, but I should warn you it's neither comfortable nor attractive.*

There is an incredibly extensive social network. One is always home-teaching, going to meetings, making Mormon crafts, or eating Jell-O.

You have the comforts of the Lord. The first comforter is Christ.

The second comforter is the Holy Ghost. *The third comforter is Jell-O.*

Music: ★ —Sickly-sweet hymns sung by the Mormon Tabernacle Choir.

Food: ★ —If you are partial to Jell-O molds that feature such exotic additions as shredded carrots, cucumbers, and canned vegetables, then this is the heaven for you! Ambrosia—Food of the Gods—is also popular. I think Jell-O infused with marshmallows in a canned-fruit and whipped cream reduction sauce is an acquired taste, probably better acquired before eternity. The blessing for Jell-O: "Please bless this food that it will strengthen and nourish our bodies." This can also be used over ice-cream, donuts, Twinkies, and Ho-Ho's.

Drink: ★ —What can you say about Postum? Ersatz alcohol, such as Martinelli's Sparkling Cider and Near Beer is available, although the rigorously righteous avoid "even the appearance of sin." However, Xanax, Vicodin and Prozac are very popular.

Accommodations: ★★ —Incredibly clean and astoundingly tacky.

Entry Requirements: ★★

OVERALL RATING: ★★

Two days or one hour later, Dirk returned to his couch. The telephone was ringing. Picking it up, he discovered that while he had been visiting the Mormons, his car too had been traveling. It had been towed to a distant auto lot, where it awaited rescue.

Cursing loudly, he took a cab to the lot, discovering that for only $200 he could reclaim his auto, which now lacked hubcaps and a radio.

"Damn that Lucifer," Dirk fumed. "Couldn't he arrange for long-term parking?"

The Antichrist

Men are better than their theology.
—Ralph Waldo Emerson

Notes:
Imagine peddling salvation door to door. Mind-boggling. I kept remembering my stint as a Fuller Brush boy; it was hard enough to sell brushes, let alone redemption.

Dirk's appearance on TV caused considerable discussion in religious and non-religious circles. The pious were outraged by the idea of multiple Heavens. The atheists were not much happier with Dirk's assertion that there was a God (or gods) and a Heaven (or heavens). And the agnostics just couldn't make up their minds.

Dirk began receiving fan mail ... of a sort. Most of the notes stated, in a variety of languages and styles, that Dirk was undoubtedly deranged, irrefutably wrong, quite possibly the Antichrist, and indubitably going to Hell. Quite a few letter-writers offered to send him there personally.

It appeared that Dirk had succeeded in accomplishing what no preceding figure in history had managed—unite all religious persuasions in one common goal: Kill Dirk Quigby.

"I don't get it," Dirk said after an evening's exertion with Angelica. "Why are they all so angry?"

"Silly," Angelica said, ruffling his hair, "you're challenging their beliefs."

"But I'm not, I'm affirming them! I'm saying there is a Heaven, and just like they've described! I'm just providing guidance for those who haven't chosen yet."

"At least half the fun of going to Heaven is knowing that all the others are going to Hell."

Colors of Creation

There are two kinds of people: those who say to God, "Thy will be done," and those to whom God says, "All right then, have it your way." —C.S. Lewis

Angelica had discovered and fallen in love with the 99-cent stores. She made regular visits to her favorites, returning home carrying bags bursting with new, exotic colors of nail polish. She painted her nails in wild colors and bold designs. She wandered through Dirk's apartment trailing waves of turpentine scent.

"During Creation," she said, "God sometimes had design competitions and let angels have some input. There was a lot of contention over humans. There were those who wanted iridescent, multicolored rainbows of people; instead, the vote narrowly came down on shades of beige and brown. Just look how badly that turned out! Then there were those who wanted humans to at least have colorful nails and hair. Women probably dye their hair and paint their nails due to an atavistic, pre-Creation sense memory." Although Angelica was never explicit about it, Dirk was fairly sure that she had voted with the colorful but losing side on the hominacea question.

"Does God still have competitions?"

"Not after his favorite left."

Angelica proudly waved a garish hand of orange, pink, and green at Dirk. "I'm showing you what you were supposed to look like."

Overall, Dirk was rather glad that her side had lost, but he took care never to mention that aloud.

And on the Seventh Day

Facts are Stupid Things.
—Ronald Reagan

D irk and Angelica were going to the movies.

Angelica loved movies. "They don't normally have films in Heaven, except in the Scientologists' pre-existence, and they were never very good. For one thing, they were unbearably long—thirty-six days to be precise."

"Wow" Dirk said, "and I thought *Berlin Alexanderplatz* was long!"

It was a chilly evening. Dirk retrieved his favorite blue pullover from the top of the dresser. Reaching his arms inside, he pulled it over his head, but as he wriggled in, the sweater appeared to grow. He strained upward, but instead of reaching light and air, he became more and more enmeshed in a world of wool. Dirk struggled and writhed to escape. When at last he emerged, sweaty and dotted with blue lint, he was standing on a cloud, in front of a pair of large wooden gates. Behind it stretched a vast expanse of lawn. Upon which people were jogging, riding horses, and doing calisthenics.

DIRK QUIGBY'S GUIDE TO THE
SEVENTH-DAY ADVENTIST AFTERLIFE

William Miller began the Seventh-day Adventist Church in 1829, fired with the conviction that Jesus *the son of God, not the Jesus Rodriguez who mows your lawn,* would return to Earth in 1844.

Unfortunately, Jesus stood them up. This is called the "Great Disappointment."

Still, you have to hand it to these folks; they are nothing if not determined. The faithful decided that even though there was clearly some mistake, "the calculations were correct, but the event was mistaken." In other words, something had happened in 1844, just not Jesus' return. What had really happened in 1844 was that Jesus had begun "an investigation" to figure out who is entitled to the "benefits of atonement" *and a permanent pension plan with dental.* When He is finished, He promises to return, probably very, very soon. Though Seventh-day Adventists refuse to disclose the exact date.

If only more people had been keeping the TRUE Saturday Sabbath and not some nasty Sunday Sabbath, the end of the world would have come in 1844 when it was supposed to.

END DESTINATION:

God exhales souls into our bodies when we are born, and inhales them back when we die. Between death and resurrection, we will not be conscious. *It would be too difficult for God to keep all those inhalations and exhalations straight.*

Both the righteous and the unrighteous dead will remain dead for a thousand years. Then the unrighteous will be briefly resurrected, judged, and destroyed in a lake of fire. *This seems like adding an awful lot to God's already-busy workload. Why not just let them remain dead?* After this, the Earth will become the abode of the righteous and the "capital of the universe." *Take that, Galileo!*

Seventh-day Adventists claim no articles of faith, creed, or discipline. But they do have an awful lot of rules. If you do not follow the rules, you will DIE!

Are we clear on that? This is the only true church of Jesus Christ.

This Heaven is less crowded than many. You are only allowed in if you have kept the Saturday Sabbath but are not a Jew. If you do not keep Saturday Sabbath, you bear the "mark of the beast." *Rather harsh, I think, considering these folks are not noted for accuracy with dates.*

ENTRY REQUIREMENTS:

Because your body is a temple you should not pollute it. No alcohol, pork, shellfish, or other unclean foods.

Remember, the road to nonexistence is paved with sex, Sangria, seafood, song, and Sunday services.

QUALITY RATINGS:

Perks: ★ ★ ★ —You don't have to go to church on Sunday. You get a "body like Christ's, delivered from defects."

Music: ★ —As with all things Adventist, there is a detailed, persnickety inventory of what makes "right thinking/listening" music. Music must be spiritual, glorify God, lack fervor and passion, and not be too loud. Stop listening. You are probably being corrupted by the sounds of Satan.

Food: ★ —Dr. J. H. Kellogg, king of Corn Flakes, was a "vigorous" *(is there any other kind?)* Seventh-day Adventist. As a result, breakfast foods and meat substitutes are very big here.

Drink: ★ —Like prune juice? You would have thought that God could have made this flawless body regular!

Accommodations: ★ ★ ★ —Kind of pretty in a rural way.

Entry Requirements: ★ ★

OVERALL RATING: ★ ★

When Dirk returned, Angelica was waiting, reading a nail polish catalogue and tapping her foot. She looked up at Dirk in obvious annoyance.

"Where have you been? We've missed the early show and …"

Dirk was tired and hungry. He had not partaken of the corn flakes and soy burgers in Heaven. He wanted a cold beer and an understanding companion. He appeared to have neither.

He strolled to the refrigerator; at least he could have the beer. Lucifer never used the same entry twice, so opening a can was probably safe. Angelica followed him.

"Well," she said, in answer to his thoughts. "There are so many ways to die, to enter Heaven. Lucifer"—she spat out the name—"probably thinks that your entry should reflect the variety."

"Humm … Nice idea, but I don't imagine many people enter Heaven through a turtleneck."

"Except for turtles," Angelica softly massaged his back with supple fingers.

Dirk sighed in contentment and sank onto the couch.

Sister Mary

Would you know my name, if I saw you in heaven?
—Eric Clapton

Notes:
Visit to Buddhist afterlife. The place was noisy with the sound of one hand clapping. Countless beings enroute to other lives and the occasional completely enlightened being on its way to nonexistence. Even being reincarnated as a wombat seems preferable to not coming back at all.

I t was a dark and stormy night. Dirk listened to his newly planted foliage rapping against the window.

Something scratched at the glass. Outside he saw a moving shadow. It was not a tree limb … Once again, something, and not a human something, was rapping at his window. Dirk inhaled sharply. Eyes narrowing he tried to make out the shape. Grabbing a vase he cautiously opened the window. Before Dirk could move; a delicate, gaunt tabby cat slipped through the gap and began twining itself, in patterns of eight, between his feet.

"Hey," Dirk said quietly, "what do you think you're doing?"

The fragile cat cocked its head up at Dirk and slowly closed one eye.

Dirk felt an unnerving thrill of recognition. Mary would often wink like that when she had made a point she considered particularly salient. The cat stared fixedly at Dirk and then, once more, winked very slowly. She opened her mouth and gave a small, almost human-sounding "merrow."

"Are you hungry, girl?" Dirk asked. "You hungry, Mary?"

He went to the kitchen, the cat trotting beside him. As he opened a can of tuna, she butted his legs, purring loudly.

Watching the cat gulp down the tuna in large, ravenous bites, Dirk remembered when Mary had been a vegetarian. Her boyfriend, Dewy McCray, had owned a vegan pet food company. Mary had proudly given out boxes of pet treats.

On the occasion of his monthly duty call to his mother, Dirk made some disparaging remarks about Dewy and his Doggie Delights.

"Well, actually the pistachio-banana-raisin chews are quite good," his mother answered.

"Mom," Dirk cried, "They're dog food."

"I read the ingredients. There's nothing in there I can't eat."

In consternation, Dirk called Mary.

"Mom is eating Dewy's Doggie Delights. She says she likes the pistachio-banana-raisin chews."

"Oh," Mary replied, "They're good, but the peanut butter-carob fudge are my favorite. Has she tried those?"

Dirk smiled to himself, watching Mary the cat wolf down her tuna. She turned, once again fixing him with her piercing eyes and slowly winked.

Tasty Treats from the Baha'i Bar and Grill

Give a man a fish and you'll feed him for a day; give him a religion, and he'll starve to death while praying for a fish. —Anonymous

Dirk and Angelica were cleaning. The once dim and dusty apartment now vibrated with color. Instead of tattered travel posters, swirling fabrics were draped in cloudlike swirls across windows and over shelves. The faded Rousseau jungles had been made bright and vibrant by Angelica, who re-tinted them with nail polish.

Dirk plugged in the vacuum. He began by annihilating the warren of dust bunnies breeding in the closet. Mary, who'd been rubbing circles between Dirk's legs, fled in horror. Dirk got into a rhythm, noting how the carpet changed hue as he pushed the fibers to and fro.

His mind wandered back through Heavens of recent memory.

It was as if people didn't want freedom. He never saw the winged dead catching thermal air currents, soaring like raptors. In many Heavens, they still spent hours on their knees in church.

Dirk unplugged the vacuum and stuck on a cornering attachment.

Animals often chose their own Paradise. One that had lots of food, and no vets. Dirk had heard rumors of a heaven where, in addition to wings, the beasts had opposable thumbs. No can was safe. Dirk wasn't sure if such a place really existed, but he enjoyed picturing it.

As he removed the brush, the vacuum turned itself on and hungrily sucked at his hand. Before he could react, his arm disappeared, the suction quickly yanking his chest, neck, and head after it.

When Dirk opened his eyes, the world seemed shrouded in a gray fog. But it was only layers of lint, dust, and hair.

Just once, I'd like to show up at Heaven's gate not looking like something the cat dragged in.

Dirk Quigby's Guide to the Baha'i Afterlife

Baha'i was founded in 1844, by Siyyid Ali-Muhammad, a Persian noble, aka "the Báb," or "The Gate."

Naturally, the Báb (and followers) were persecuted and captured by the Islamic clergy.

Although the Báb patiently explained that he was not yet finished teaching, he was rudely suspended from a barracks wall. As thousands watched, hundreds of rifles fired. When the smoke cleared, the Báb had vanished.

When the authorities found him, he was giving final instructions to his followers.

This time, *the squad had bullets in their guns.* As usual, bloody persecution ensued.

However, the Báb had alluded to a Promised One, or "He whom God shall make manifest." Over the next twenty years, more than twenty-five people claimed to be the Promised One.

Subh-i-Azal won. Subh-i-Azal generally spent time in Baghdad hiding, wearing disguises and disavowing allegiance to the Báb whenever necessary. Ten years later Bahá'u'lláh revealed that he was the Real Promised One. *Oops.*

Unlike prophets past, Baha'u'llah did not hire holy ghost writers. He wrote many books, like *The Book of Certitude* and *The Most Holy Book.* These were followed by *The Second Most Holy Book, Not the Most Holy, but Nonetheless a Very Holy Book, A Not Very Holy Book,* and

Recipes and Tasty Treats from the Baha'i Bar and Grill.

The writings contain a blueprint for world civilization and cover everything from the treatment of animals to world government *and delicious concoctions.*

There is a tad of unfriendliness to nonbelievers: non-Baha'i's are forbidden to live in five central Iranian provinces. Their property can be confiscated. Their holy places are to be demolished. And all non-Baha'i books should be destroyed. But these words were never taken seriously: "It is ... a game, never ... intended to be put into practice." *I remember that game from P.E.*

END DESTINATION:

Heaven and Hell are not places but states of being.

In the afterlife, the soul separates from the body and journeys toward God. Getting close to God is like what Heaven would be, if there were a Heaven. Distance from God is what Hell would be, if there were a Hell.

The spiritual world is a timeless and placeless extension of our universe. Everyone will eventually get to the state of mind which is Heaven.

ENTRY REQUIREMENTS:

If you're a Star Trek fan and like the Federation, this is the religion for you! Although you will eventually reach a heavenly state of mind, why wait? Let's make Heaven here and now. We'll establish a universal language, system of weights and measures, and compulsory education. We'll abolish poverty, wealth, and form a world federation ensuring lasting peace. *Would Captain Kirk feel at home here or what?!*

Even Baha'i holidays are inclusive, e.g., "World Religion Day" and "Race Unity Day." The Baha'i New Year marks the end of a nineteen-day sunrise-to-sunset fast *known as the Baha'i diet. Much more effective than the Scarsdale Diet.* Spend *mealtimes* in prayer and meditation.

There is only one God and one human family, *despite all evidence to the contrary,* every religion serves God.

There is no such thing as "original sin." People are intrinsically good. Evil is not within our nature. *Studying history is not within our nature.*

Evil is the absence of good, just as darkness is the absence of light; it has no independent existence. Satan is just a symbol and should not be taken literally. *Satan objects to this, claiming he is just as real as God.*

Knowledge of right and wrong can be obtained by following the teachings of the prophets.

QUALITY RATINGS:

Perks: ★ ★ ★ —If you enjoy community gatherings and grassroots organizations, you'll love this place. You can be a wee bit smug about how advanced you are.

Music: ★ ★ ★ —A variety of alternative soft rock/folk devotional ditties. Like Yanni with a sitar. I was told it was the music of the spheres; you hear what you want to hear. If you like rap, or heavy metal, it's hell.

Food: ★ ★ ★ —I was not served anything; everyone was too busy striving toward spiritual perfection to bother cooking. But I hear the Baha'i Bar & Grill serves a good lacto-*vegan* sandwich.

Drink: ★ ★ —See food.

Accommodations: ★ ★ ★ ★ —One is wandering around feeling euphoric all the time. Besides, since you're lacking a body, who cares?

Entry Requirements: ★ ★ ★ ★

OVERALL RATING: ★ ★ ★ ★

Dirk returned to the couch two days later. Baha'i heaven had left him feeling full and content.

"So where did you go?" Angelica asked. She perched on the arm of the couch, Kahlua with caramel-strawberry-chocolate milkshake in hand.

"I was in Baha'i heaven, at last a heaven that seems like Heaven. Oh, not in the usual sense—there were no golden harps or winged beings, no transoms into Hell to view the torments of the damned. I was welcomed in, even though I was encased in lint. They judge not."

"Lest ye be judged," Angelica finished.

"No, they judge not because they don't care. 'Judge not, lest ye be judged' is mandating compassion through fear.

"In Baha'i heaven, they are trying to get to perfection, and they know you are too. They want you to be successful. It's as if you were going to a fabulous party and wanted your friends there. You'd give them directions because you genuinely desired their presence, not because you feared punishment if they got lost en route."

"Wow, I've never seen you this enthusiastic before. Are you going to convert?"

Dirk hesitated. "I'm not ready to convert to anything," he replied slowly. "The only thing I didn't like about the place was that they seemed a little smug, a tad full of themselves. Still, I much prefer Heavens that don't care if you convert or not. I always believed that God, if there was a God, wouldn't be, couldn't be so petty as to send you to eternal damnation because you had not had some water drops sprinkled over you by a priest. Then there are all these Heavens for people immersed in total immersion. Is God really going to send you to Hell because one of your feet didn't get doused in the baptismal font? Though actually," Dirk mused, "from what I've seen of the world, that's just the kind of unfair, nonsensical, arbitrary thing that the Creator might do. Where is God, anyway?"

Angelica sipped her shake. "I imagine you've seen God. He probably wasn't what you expected. He's a busy guy, you know. Doesn't really have time to hang out with a bunch of losers attempting to play harps and fly, even though they're tone deaf and suffer a fear of heights. Let me assure you, an airsick angel is not a pretty sight."

"I've seen God? When, where?"

"Well … I can almost guarantee you, he wasn't sitting on a throne counting sparrows—he leaves all the bird counts to those fanatics in the Audubon Angels Association. Have some Kahlua."

Dirk raised his glass, "Here's to an accepting God, a cream-choked cat, liver-coated canaries, and Audubon Angels."

By Any Other Name

I simply haven't the nerve to imagine a being, a force, a cause which keeps the planets revolving in their orbits, and then suddenly stops in order to give me a bicycle with three speeds. —Quentin Crisp

Notes:
In the East, it's noblemen who are prophets (Buddha, Muhammad, the Báb, etc.) while in the West and Middle East, it's a more plebeian career (Joseph Smith, Mary Baker Eddy, Jesus Christ etc.)

The Báb was born in Persia, which turned into Iran ... How does a country change names, wondered Dirk.

As usual, although he had not spoken aloud, Angelica answered him.

"From 600 BC to AD 1935, Iran was known as Persia to outsiders. But inside Persia, ever since the Sassanid period (226–651) which is either the third Iranian dynasty or the second Persian Empire, depending on how you slice the falafel, Persians called their country 'Iran' meaning 'the land of Aryans.' 'Arya' means 'Noble' in Sanskrit and refers to Kings and rulers from India, and China.

"Persians/Iranians claim they're descendents of the Aryans, you know. Well, in 1935 Nazi Germany was buddying up to nations of 'Aryan' blood ... or anyone who might help them take over the world. German friends of the Persian soon-to-be-Iranian ambassador convinced him that Persia, now free of the nasty influence of Britain and Russia, should be called Iran. This would not only signal a new beginning, but would also proclaim its Aryan-ness, and might even make the Persians blond and blue-eyed."

"But I don't get it," Dirk said, "Surely the kings of India, Sri Lanka, and China weren't blue-eyed and blond-haired? Come to think of it I haven't seen many blond, blue-eyed Iranians either."

"Have you ever seen Hitler?" Angelica asked. "Not exactly an Aryan poster boy, is he?"

Dirk laughed.

Cats and Dogs

The road to hell is paved with good Samaritans.
—William M. Holden

Dirk found it amusing that Mary had become a carnivore; she had been such a dedicated vegetarian.

Actually, the dedication had been mostly evident on the side of her then-boyfriend, Dewy C. McCray. Dewy was a conceptual artist and indie film director. He had the vision of a painter and the soul of a poet. In other words, he was myopic and self-absorbed. Due to the public's lack of sensitivity, he could not support himself on concept alone. He made his money from his pet food company, which specialized in vegan pet treats for dogs and cats. Dewy marketed "Dalai Lama Doggie Delights," "Toto's Tofu Treats," "Spot's Soy Snacks," and "Carrot Cat Chews," to pet boutiques in most major cities.

"Cats against Carnivores" and "Predators for Peace" read the brightly colored bumper stickers that Dewy distributed with his pet treats.

Unfortunately, cats that don't eat meat grow blind. This, however, did not stop the entrepreneurial Dewy. He simply began a subsidiary business, "Dewy's Seeing Eye Dogs for Blind, Kind Cats." He hoped this would not only aid the blind but promote interspecies harmony. It was an unfortunate side effect that some of the Seeing Eye dogs ate their charges. Revolutions are never without casualties.

In his spare time, Dewy was an activist and crusader for animal rights. He would drive out into the countryside, steal into mink farms—cleverly wearing a mink coat as a disguise—and let loose the minks of war. The minks raced, slithered, and slunk to freedom, where they hungrily depopulated the surrounding area with a speed and voracity that would have surprised and saddened him had he stayed around to see. Dewy, however, after having carefully concealed his mink coat in the trunk of his new Hummer (environmentally upholstered in vinyl), was already racing back to the city to plot another deliverance.

Dewy and his cohorts, MINKs (Mammals Inclined to Natural Kindness), released many minks. Mary was not normally party to Dewy's emancipation efforts, but due to a sudden allergy attack of one of MINKs' members, Dewy convinced Mary to act as a stand-in.

Unfortunately, in his haste to pursue liberty, Dewy accidentally grabbed directions to the Training Academy for Seeing Eye and Guard Dogs. Even more unfortunately, he had broken into the Doberman intruder training section.

Although the dogs had not yet completed the course, they nonetheless attacked with vigor. Dewy lost his right ear in the melee. Indeed, he only managed to escape with his life by cleverly rubbing steak sauce (which he carried in his pocket to entice the minks) on Mary and throwing her in front of him, thus providing a distracting snack for the voracious Dobermans.

The horror of this experience, as well as the bloodlust of his hitherto furry-friends, embittered Dewy. He changed his name to Kim, moved to Korea, and opened a restaurant specializing in dog fricassee. For all Dirk knew, Kim/Dewy might be there even now.

The Matrix

I don't know why we are here, but I'm pretty sure that it is not in order to enjoy ourselves. —Ludwig Wittgenstein

Dirk had just finished showering. He toweled off, humming contentedly to himself. Life was better than it had been in a very long time. He was in love, traveling, making his living writing, and Mary had returned, although he could not actually talk to her. Well, he could talk to her; he just couldn't understand her replies. Still, he could imagine her part of the conversation. It was amazing how completely they agreed nowadays. Very occasionally, she would growl or stalk off in high dudgeon, but it was rare.

And it was a continual, considerable relief to know that there was life after death. All you needed was belief.

True, Dirk thought as he reached for his blow dryer, *I haven't yet found my personal paradise, but that might come. Perhaps I could be a peripatetic soul, like Angelica. I could—*

Whoosh! The stream of air became a whirlwind, blowing him across the room, sucking him in circles, reeling him in, in, in.

He awoke encased in a fine, viscous mist. He felt surrounded by souls but could see nothing.

He was in the realm of the Christian Scientists.

DIRK QUIGBY'S GUIDE TO THE CHRISTIAN SCIENCE AFTERLIFE

Mary Baker Eddy is the only Western woman to found a worldwide religion.

Born in New England, she was an unhealthy child, raised in a devout Calvinist family. *No wonder she started a new religion.* A sickly adult, she became a patient of Phineas Parkhurst Quimby, who believed illness and death only existed in the mind. In 1866, *his mind caught a horrible cold and he died.*

A few weeks after Quimby's death, Ms. Eddy slipped on an icy sidewalk, striking her back and suffering internal injuries. She was told that she would never walk again and would die a slow, painful death. *Her physician was famous throughout Calvinist New England for his inspiring, cheerful bedside manner.* But while reading her Bible, Mary felt God's presence and was cured.

She spent the next three years trying to figure out what had happened, and the rest of her life developing the "Science of Christianity," referred to by nonbelievers to as neither Christian nor science.

Mary Baker Eddy explains Christian Science in *Science and Health with Key to the Scriptures.* The elegance and brevity of the title *will give you a fairly accurate idea of her writing style.*

In her eighty-eighth year, she founded the *Christian Science Monitor.*

END DESTINATION:

Heaven and Hell are both states of mind. The material world does not really exist. Death does not really exist. *Please ignore all the corpses in the cemetery.*

After death, you will realize that death is a lie. *This leads to a Heaven full of awfully befuddled folks, but no matter. Matter, after all is false.*

ENTRY REQUIREMENTS:

This afterlife is perfect for fans of "The Matrix." The main belief is that the material world has no substance and is a distortion of reality, a waking dream.

Given the absolute goodness and perfection of God, it's obvious that sin, disease, and death were not created by Him and are not real. Evil and its manifestations are terrible lies about God and His creation.

You'd think if material things lack reality, it wouldn't matter what you do with them ... wrong! Wrong, wrong, wrong. You can't engage in activities that impede your ability to pray, so no drugs, alcohol, or tobacco. Christian Scientists also eschew regular medicine, for if illness is false, how can doctors be real?

It should be noted the members are not forbidden doctors, although they are scorned for being spiritual pansies.

Sunday service consists of hymns, prayer, and readings from both the King James Bible and *Science and Health with Key to the Scriptures*. The twenty-six topics for sermons follow in unchanging order dictated by Eddy, *who was apparently a control freak. Make sure you have a new edition of "Science and Health" or suffer death by typo.*

The Church has no clergy.

There is a weekly Wednesday meeting, where members share their miraculous cures. *My favorite testimony came from the formerly legless three-legged man.*

QUALITY RATINGS:

Perks: ★ ★ ★ ★ —You will never have to go to a doctor or emergency room, receive a colonoscopy, mammogram, Pap smear, or surgery. *That alone made me ready to sign up!*

Music: ★ ★ —Imagine a soundless sound, a voice without a throat.

Food: ★★ —Because the material is false (it lacks substance), I never felt full here.

Drink: ★★ —See food.

Accommodations: ★★★★ —If you like being a spirit, you will love this place.

Entry Requirements: ★★★

OVERALL RATING: ★★★

Of Cats and Kin

"What is there in this world that truly makes living worthwhile?"
Death thought about it. "Cats," he said eventually, "Cats are nice."
—Terry Pratchett

It was a peaceful Saturday morning. Dirk lay in bed, Angelica by his side, Mary at his feet. Dirk felt content and relaxed, sandwiched between the females he loved.

He lazily reached down, scratching Mary gently behind the ears. Purring, loudly she looked adoringly up at him and slowly winked.

"It really doesn't prove anything, you know," Angelica growled. "Just because she winks like your sister doesn't mean she is your sister."

"Wouldn't you, an angel, know if she was Mary?"

"Not necessarily. If she's a cat in this life, then she's a cat. I really don't see why you have to feed her tuna and chicken."

"Mom always told me to look after Mary. Didn't she, Mary?" Dirk said. He stroked the delicate calico.

Mary looked up smugly at Angelica, whose teeth elongated.

In spite of Angelica, Dirk had become more and more convinced that Mary was his sister. Her way of winking, cleaning her nails, and stretching luxuriously were all more than slightly reminiscent of Mary.

Love Letters

The light at the end of the tunnel is just the light of an oncoming train.
—Robert Lowell

It was a beautiful day. Dirk opened his door intending to water his garden. On the stoop rested a square carton, neatly wrapped in brown paper and addressed, to "Mr. Dirk Quigby." Considering that the majority of Dirk's mail lately had been addressed to "the antichrist," "De Anti CHrIst," "The Devil's spawn," and "The Abortion that should have been," Dirk felt relieved. But bending to retrieve the package, the peace was shattered by a heart-stopping wail.

"Shit!" Dirk, dropped the packet on the floor. Mary crouched on the floor, eyes wide, pupils dilated, an unearthly cry issuing from her throat. "What's wrong, girl?" Mary continued howling.

Angelica emerged from the bedroom, covering her ears, her teeth lengthening to a degree that Dirk had never seen before. It was at moments like these that he most questioned their relationship.

Angelica eyed the cat dangerously. She inhaled deeply. "Someone doesn't like you, Dirk," she hissed.

Dirk was still trying to figure out if that someone she was referring to was herself or Mary, when Angelica laid a long-fingered hand over the packet. Immediately it began to writhe, fizzle, and hiss, a bit like a disgruntled electric blanket. The wrapping curled off the package and a bewildering assortment of wires disconnected themselves from a glinting metallic panel, leaving the bomb dismembered though still writhing on the floor. Dirk inhaled sharply.

The stench of burnt wires and thwarted hatred filled the room. At least that is what Dirk assumed thwarted hatred would smell like.

To say that Dirk was disturbed would be an understatement of the highest order. He was beyond disturbed, well into the region of shock and disbelief.

Why was he so hated? Why was everyone so angry? He was only reporting the conditions in the Heavens that they themselves had created.

To distract himself, he took Angelica shopping. He dropped her off at a nail polish emporium that she had read about and longed to visit.

"They have colors in ultraviolet that only bees can see! And ones in the infrared that can only be seen by certain fish, snakes, camcorders, and," she modestly lowered her eyes, "angels."

"Well, who invented them, and why?" He was disturbed by the letter bomb, and the ultra-infrared polish provided no solace. "What is the point of nail polish you can't see?"

"*I* can see it. You can't."

While Angelica pursued polish, Dirk visited a pet store. He bought "Tartar Control Kaviar," and "DUI Catnip."

Returning home, Angelica enthusiastically began decorating herself and various other objects with her new polish. Dirk much preferred the invisible colors to visible ones. The only irritant was the smell, but higher prices have been paid for love.

Dirk sought to placate Mary, who was much more scent-sensitive. He had bought her a scratching post—more of a scratching box really. It was a thick piece of corrugated cardboard, about an inch high. Dirk opened the round plastic container of "DUI Catnip" and rubbed it into the board. Mary nosed the nip and rolled on her back in ecstasy. She made little mews of pleasure and looked up at Dirk flirtatiously. Mary butted his hand, then returned to rolling. Eventually she ate some, and soon was sleeping, curled on her side, belly up, deep in catnip dreams.

"You always liked your pot, didn't you, girl?" Dirk cooed, fondly rubbing her tummy.

"You may find animal intoxication cute and junkies endearing, but I do not," Angelica said huffily. She stalked out of the room with a catlike hauteur.

Why, Dirk thought *is being in the dog house so very different from being in the cat house? It's not as though she's a puritan. She likes her wine just fine ... She's no angel, figuratively speaking.* Dirk sighed and rubbed Mary's exposed soft white stomach. She purred in her sleep.

Annihilation

*My young son asked me what happens after we die. I told him we get
buried under a bunch of dirt and worms eat our bodies. I guess I should
have told him the truth—that most of us go to Hell and burn eternally—
but I didn't want to upset him.* —Jack Handey

Dirk was nervous. As usual, he was waiting around to be sucked into
a bottle, consumed by an air vent, or pulled into a box of Kleenex.
He needed a cigarette. He pulled open his desk, and something grabbed
his hand. His body tensed and yanked backward ... His finger sported
looped metal headgear, looking like a demented New Age finger puppet.
He'd been snatched by a paper clip.

Laughing sheepishly, Dirk removed the clip and nervously returned
to groping in his desk. He pulled out a cigarette and lit it.

Swoosh! The flame leaped up. He felt the familiar tightening in his
solar plexus.

That filthy Devil, Dirk thought, but nothing happened. He waited a
bit, breathing hard.

Impatient and frustrated, he decided to take a jog. Usually, he didn't
run unless something large and vicious was chasing him. Tonight, however, he needed the release.

As he ran the wind fanned his face and wiped all thought from his
mind. He sped through the dirty city streets, enjoying the sensation of
speed when ... *Shoosh!* He flew through the air, a wingless angel. Landing
hard, he looked up, expecting to see Heaven's Gate. But he was lying on
the sidewalk, hands scraped and knees skinned. Looking over his shoulder, he noticed a pothole.

Limping home, he hobbled toward the shower. Warm beads of water washed away sweat and fear. But as he reached for the soap, he felt his body twisting, whirling, and condensing down, down, down, into the black wetness of the drain.

He awoke nude and dripping, in front of a golden gate, which proudly read, No Vacancy.

Dirk Quigby's Guide to the Jehovah's Witness Afterlife

Most Jehovah's Witnesses don't get to Heaven. Heaven has a housing shortage. Actually, heaven's always been full, but after Lucifer's rebellion, all 144,000 fallen angels' apartments opened up.

The available apartments will be filled on Judgment Day. And *The Watchtower*, the Jehovah's Witnesses' magazine (now available on DVD), publishes definite dates for the end of the world, and it publishes them often. The end of the world and Christ's return was predicted for 1873, 1874, 1914, 1925, and 1975. Now it is generally agreed that Christ has already arrived but is invisible.

End Destination:

One hundred forty-four thousand lucky souls will go to Heaven. Other observant Jehovah's Witnesses will reside on a refurbished Earth.

TOTAL, COMPLETE ANNIHILATION for the rest.

Entry Requirements:

Believe in Christ the Resurrected Spirit and God the Father. The Trinity is a wrong, evil notion, and will result in total, complete annihilation.

Unless you hanker to join the Dodo, follow the rules of this, the only true church of Jesus Christ.

Jesus is not God. Before Jesus lived on Earth, he was the Arch-angel Michael. *Which makes me wonder who that angel I met last week calling himself Michael was.*

On Earth, Michael/Jesus was a man who lived a perfect life; *and sold more "Watchtowers" than anyone—especially admirable because this was before the printing press.*

Jesus died on a stake and was resurrected as a spirit. *Easier than resurrecting an entire body.*

We, however, will be resurrected bodies intact. Believe that only the soul is resurrected, and both your body and soul will be destroyed.

Don't celebrate holidays.

Birthday celebrations are not allowed because two pagans killed people on their birthdays … The pharaoh killed his baker *although if you had tasted his eggplant casserole* … King Herod killed John the Baptist. So if you have a birthday party you will be annihilated *and not get any presents.*

Jesus was born in early October. The exact date is unknown because God doesn't like birthday parties … as should be clear by now. If you can't get this simple, itty-bitty fact into your head, you *deserve* annihilation.

"We do not partake of a pagan celebration of his birth when he was not born yet then!" *Well put!*

Shun heathen rituals like Thanksgiving and Easter.

If you give blood or get blood, (blood is sacred to GOD aka Jehovah, and should not be used for such frivolous things like surger-ies or transfusions), attend proms, vote or salute the flag (idolatry), read *Harry Potter*, mention anything to do with "fate," own a Smurf, or eat Lucky Charms—you will be completely annihilated.

It's even a no-no to buy Girl Scout Cookies. *I'd really miss Thin Mints.*

You are only allowed to take part in communion if you are part of the elite group of 144,000. Partake at your own risk.

If you believe in hell rather than TOTAL, COMPLETE, ANNIHILATION, you will be totally and completely annihilated.

If you make it back to Earth, you must obey God perfectly for a thousand years. Remember, it's never too late for annihilation.

QUALITY RATINGS:
Perks: ★ —You'll never lose a game, because they are forbidden.
   You'll get a lot of outdoor exercise, handing out *Watchtowers*.
   It won't matter if you don't get invited to parties or dances.
Food: ★★ —Like fried chicken & mashed potatoes?
Drink: ★ —How does none grab you?
Music: ★ —Music, like children, is better seen than heard.
Accommodations: ★★★★ —Nice gardens on Earth; an excess of gold and white in Heaven.
Entry Requirements: ★
OVERALL RATING: ★

Dirk awoke on his couch, two hours or three weeks later, still draped in the white robes he'd been given in heaven. This time, instead of sinking into soft pillows, he materialized on top of Angelica. She'd been propped up on the couch; legs spread, white cotton balls wedged like smashed, captive clouds between her toes. She'd been applying arcs of metallic magenta over her bright yellow toenails.

"Ow!" Angelica screamed, kicking up her legs, propelling Dirk and the open vials of polish across the room.

"Shit!" Dirk and Angelica stood staring at each other, eyes wide. They stood frozen for a moment, then began laughing.

Dirk was relieved. Often Angelica failed to see the humor of mishaps, especially if it involved her nails. This time, however, they both seemed infected by similar strains of hysteria. They whooped, snorted, howled, and shrieked, tears streaming down their cheeks.

"I can't breathe," Dirk sobbed.

"Ohhhh …" Angelica exhaled. "You scared the shit out of me! Where in hell did you spring from?"

"Not Hell … although …" He wiped his eyes with the back of his shirtsleeve.

"Disappointed?"

"Well, I'm conflicted. I mean, I have yet to visit my ideal Heaven, but some of these places … They aren't what I imagined, if I dared to imagine. At first, I was just grateful that there *was* an afterlife. I was, I am, filled with relief that we, that I, will not cease to exist—though in some of the Eastern heavens, the ideal is nonexistence.

"But people seem so unchanged. Just as petty and full of hate as they were on Earth …"

"'On Earth as it is in Heaven,'" Angelica quoted. "You get what you pay for; or rather you get what you pray for. If you have created a belief based on an all-forgiving God who punishes eternally for a 'sin' committed during a paltry twenty to seventy years of being—you have lovely hair," she said, ruffling her hands through his thick brown mane. She kissed his nose. "God has a much more advanced sense of humor than you critters give him credit for. Just look at the duckbilled platypus."

"Ha, ha," Dirk said "That God guy is such a kidder. It's especially funny when He creates those famines in India."

"Now, now," Angelica stroked his hair, "If your species showed a little more restraint about reproducing …"

"Talking about reproducing," Dirk breathed into her ear. "What'd you say to a little hybrid interaction?"

Angelica replied with a kiss.

"Now that's what I call talking in tongues."

Eden

God, protect me from your followers.
—Anonymous

Dirk was digging in his runty strip of garden. Angelica displayed no interest in growing things, although she had contributed color by planting some plastic pink flamingos, whose color she had enhanced by the ubiquitous nacre of nail polish.

Dirk dug in the dirt, planting a sweet potato that had rooted while awaiting baking. The potato had hidden in the back of a cupboard. Dirk discovered it displaying nascent roots and a single blind white stem, attempting to put forth leaves, fragile as tissue and pale as ivory. The valiant attempt of the sweet potato, growing without light, soil, or water moved Dirk. Cradling it in his hands, he carried it outside. He was considering asking Angelica to water it, so as to avoid another encounter with a voracious garden hose, but as Lucifer never seemed to use the same means of transport twice, he decided against it. Placing the potato in the dirt, Dirk spread its feeble roots into the hole.

He straightened up, dusting soil from his hands. It was a warm day, and rivulets of sweat dripped down his back. He wanted a shower, but felt panicky, fearful of being sucked into another afterlife.

He risked a shower, but as he soaped, tiny hands squeezed his intestines.

If it's justified is it paranoia?

Any time he wanted beer, music, a shower, or needed to touch anything, his body went rigid. He could no longer tell the difference between tension and transformation.

Emerging from the bathroom, Dirk discovered Lucifer, sitting on the couch, puffing a cheroot. The smell of vanilla, bourbon, and anisette filled the room. Luckily, Angelica was out.

"I wish you'd give me some warning when I'm about to depart for an afterlife," Dirk said, searching in his pocket for a cigarette.

"No one knows when they go to the next life," Lucifer said. "I've already bent all kinds of natural laws for you. I'm not breaking this one."

"I'm living in fear," Dirk complained. "Are you sure you can't give me some warning?"

"We've been over this before," Lucifer sighed. "Everyone should live as if they might depart for the afterlife at any moment. Consider yourself lucky."

"Oh yeah, real luck," Dirk said, lighting up. "I show up covered in lint, ice-cream, or beer, soaking wet and holding my dick—just how everyone wants to visit Heaven. I'm giving reporters a bad reputation."

"Don't worry," Lucifer said. "I doubt that's possible."

Electrical Attractions

*God was my co-pilot, but we crashed in the mountains
and I had to eat him.* —Anonymous

Notes:
Wednesday: Was supposed to go to the Wiccan Heaven. I assumed they
wouldn't let men enter, and I refused to wear a dress. But I'm told that
Wicca does allow male members ... if they have very small members and
agree to pee sitting down.
Humiliating enough that I have to wear blackface to visit the Nation of
Islam.

Dirk's computer had been cleverly programmed to implode whenever
the words "God," "Christ," "Muhammad," or "Mohammad" were
typed, thereby adroitly obscuring the hacker's religion, as well as ensuring that Dirk would be annihilated during an act of apostasy. But due
perhaps to the almost continual presence of spiritual, hence unnatural,
vibrations in his apartment, this did not happen.

Indeed, Dirk was not at the computer, nor was the computer on,
when it began to make querulous, crackling noises.

Dirk looked at his whimpering, clucking machine. As he approached,
it began to smoke.

Mary emitted a heartrending wail, leapt at his leg, and embedded her
front claws in his jeans. She continued producing a hysterical, if rather
muffled, howl.

Angelica entered hastily. Although she claimed that Mary was nothing but a cat (and a rather unpleasant and spoiled cat at that), she seemed nonetheless almost esoterically connected to Mary's ambiance; of course, the howling might have had some effect as well.

"Don't touch it!"

Ignoring her own advice, Angelica crossed over to the gibbering machine and extended her hand. The machine exploded in an impressive burst of fire. Angelica burst into flames, vanishing in a cloud of black, acrid smoke.

★

In spite of her name and heritage, Angelica wasn't always an angel. Dirk found her hostility toward Mary upsetting, her jealousy of Lucifer childish, and her capricious dental span downright repulsive.

Still, she was his main and only squeeze. On occasion, he even loved her.

★

The room was cold. The air thick. Breath suspended. She had died protecting him. Angelica. His angel.

As the smoke cleared. Dirk, stared through tear-blurred eyes at Angelica. Her hair looked softer and more lustrous. Her glasses seemed to have melted away, revealing lovely gray-green eyes. Her mouth appeared lusher, her figure more curved and voluptuous.

"It's the electricity," she purred, noticing his scrutiny. "It's present in the human heart, you know. It's how we keep track of our charges. Angels find it … um … very … refreshing … God never planned for so much interference—so much stray voltage—when he designed the system. There's nothing like a good meltdown to give us angels a buzz." A narrow pink tongue poked out and licked her voluptuous lips. She gave a positively post-coital smile.

Of God and Ganja

Reality is just a crutch for people who can't deal with drugs. —Lily Tomlin

Dirk was considerably shaken by the increasing frequency of attempts to end his life. In some ways, the fact that someone—and more than one someone—despised him enough to kill was more disturbing than the explosions. What had he done to engender such hate? All his life Dirk had wanted to be loved, or liked—or at least ignored.

"It's okay to visit, but I wouldn't want to die there," he confessed to Angelica over after-dinner cognac.

"Which is your favorite?"

"Philosophically, Baha'i and Quakers hands down, even the Jews and Christian Scientists aren't so bad—any place that accepts you regardless of earthly affiliations is okay by me. But for a good time, I'd recommend the Garden of Paradise every time."

"If you're a man," Angelica said. She looked hostilely at the empty bottle.

Dirk offered to run to the store for Kahlua, cognac, ice-cream, and chocolate. Besides, he was out of cigarettes. Giving her a kiss, he grabbed his wallet and jumped in the car, barely feeling his single cognac. He made his purchases and headed home, unaware of the black-and-white cruiser stealthily following.

Dirk had driven only a quarter of a block when he was blinded by light and deafened by shrill yodeling. Pulling over, he blinked like an owl at the unsmiling policeman leaning in his open window.

"Get out of the car. Let me see your license and registration," the man in blue demanded.

Dirk hesitated; his registration was in the glove compartment. If he got out of the car, he wouldn't be able to hand it to the cop, because it would be in the car.

The officer sniffed. "Have you been drinking?"

Dirk attempted an ingratiating smile, attempting to convey admiration for those who "protect and serve."

"Out," the cop snapped, extending his hand for Dirk's documents.

Dirk reached over and opened his glove compartment, reaching for his registration.

"Hands in the air," the officer shouted, pulling out his pistol.

Before Dirk could comply, the registration had grabbed his fingers and rapidly sucked him into the snug darkness of the glove compartment.

Dirk had never been so glad to get to Heaven in his life.

He was standing in a modest village. Grass huts were scattered among verdant fields, sparkling crystal rivers and magnificent foaming falls dotted the countryside. Exotic animals leaped about, barely visible through the heavy, sweet haze that filled the air. Although Dirk could not quite place the scent, it made him nostalgic.

Glancing up at the entryway through which he had been peering, Dirk read these words: *"The darker the skin, the quicker you're in."*

Dirk gazed doubtfully at his pale hands.

DIRK QUIGBY'S GUIDE TO THE RASTAFARI AFTERLIFE

Note: Rastafari is sometimes called "Rastafarianism." This is considered improper and offensive. Rastas reject "isms and schisms." Academics reject their rejection and continue to use the term.

END DESTINATION:

The elite will live forever in their current bodies (*better get in shape now*), in Ethiopia.

Believe that blacks are Jews. Jamaica is Babylon. Ethiopia is Heaven. Emperor Haile Selassie is God. Smoking massive amounts of ganja is an act of faith.

God commanded: "Thou shalt eat the herb of the field," *in brownies.*

Ras Tafari was crowned King of Ethiopia in 1930 and became the Emperor Haile Selassie, "Lord of Lords and King of Kings of Ethiopia, Conquering Lion of the Tribe of Judah, the Elect of God and the Light of the World." (*If only Napoleon had had Haile Selassie's press agent … "Lord of Lords and King of Kings" makes "Emperor" seem so pathetic.*) The Rastas, in spite of vehement protests from Haile Selassie (a staunch Christian), declared him God. *That must have been some good shit.*

Although Haile Selassie has reportedly died, do not believe it. It is a scam by the evil white media to try to destroy the faith. In reality Haile Selassie now sits on the highest point of Mount Zion.

Haile Selassie is a reincarnation of Jesus. He is God the Father and the Son. We are the Holy Spirit.

Blacks are descendants of the twelve tribes of Israel cast from Ethiopia (Paradise) as a result of the evils of Babylon (Jamaica and the slave trade).

Only half of the Bible has been written, and the other half (stolen along with most of black culture) is written in a man's heart. *The lost half of the Bible and the whole of stolen black culture can be found next to the Ark of the Covenant (a repository of African wisdom), the Ten Commandments, and the genuine Shroud of Turin in the Lost Artifacts of God Museum.*

Rastafari is not centralized. Individual Rastafari must take their own tokes and work out their own truths.

Marcus Garvey, though Greek Orthodox, is a Prophet.

Rasta colors are red for the Church Triumphant and the blood of martyrs, with green and yellow for the fertility and wealth of Ethiopia, the Promised Land.

To be a good Rasta, follow the simple, natural life that Babylon tried to destroy.

No milk, coffee, alcohol, or soft drinks.

Stash oodles of organic treats to satisfy the munchies.

Grow dreadlocks, which symbolize the Lion of Judah, rebellion against Babylon, and *savings on shampoo*.

Connect with an abundance of women, thus producing an abundance of Rastafarianitos.

Don't bogart joints.

Gays are products of Babylon and should be exterminated *if you're not too mellowed out.*

There are two types of ceremonies. "Reasoning" is when Rastas gather, smoke ganja, and discuss ethical, social, and religious issues (*slowly and repeatedly*). The bong is passed clockwise. The second sort of ceremony is a "Binghi," or "Grounation," which is celebrated by dancing, ganja, singing, ganja, feasting, ganja and ganja, ganja. It can last for several days and seems a lot longer. Important dates include Bob Marley's birthday, Emperor Haile Selassie's birthday, Marcus Garvey's birthday *and boy is that birthday cake tasty!*

Time seemed to pass very slowly here. I forgot what I was about to write, but it was nuanced, deep, and spiritual.

QUALITY RATINGS:
Perks: ★ ★ ★ —You never have a "bad hair" day.

Like ganja?

This place pulses; dancers will love it.

Food: ★ ★ ★ ★ ★   —Organic. It tasted GREAT!

Drink: ★ ★ ★   —Water and juice, it tasted GREAT!

Music: ★ ★ ★ ★   —Reggae. Throbbing, beating, pulsing Reggae! I became part of the music! I experienced music as color and light.

Nyabinghi music is the most traditional form of Rasta music. It includes drumming, chanting, and dancing, along with prayer and pot. Bob Marley and Peter Tosh rule!

Accommodations: ★ ★ ★   —All-natural huts. If you've had enough ganja, it's all good.

Entry Requirements:

For blacks: ★ ★ ★ ★

For whites: ★

OVERALL RATING: ★ ★ ★ (for men only, as usual.)

When Dirk returned fifteen minutes or two weeks later, he had trouble focusing on the clock.

When he had disappeared, the policeman fainted, leaving his partner to call in an abandoned-car report. Neither officer opted to investigate the strange case of the hungry glove compartment. They had been so flustered by Dirk's vanishing act that they had not ticketed his car or even remembered to confiscate the Kahlua and cognac as evidence. Angelica had retrieved his car.

Dirk could not recall when he had left for Rasta Heaven. What did it matter anyway? Time was relative; colors, sensation, ideas, were all that mattered. Mary, who had been clawing the catnip post, gazed up at him, pupils dilated, her eyes wild and black. She took one final sniff, ate a few mouthfuls, and jumped up beside him. Dirk stroked her now-sleek coat. Mary purred and licked his nose.

Dirk felt quietly yet intensely content with the entire world, this one and the next. He scratched Mary under the chin and she purred.

Outside the Box

I can't go back to yesterday—because I was a different person then.
—Lewis Carroll

Dirk awoke, mind clear of Rasta Smoke. He began to wonder ... Wonder about Angelica's electrical impulses. Wonder about the uncountable computer crashes he and everyone he knew had experienced. Who or what was responsible?

He looked at Angelica.

"Well, it's hard to get good electricity these days," she countered defensively.

Dirk remembered the space shuttle explosion. Some had proposed that God was angry because it was not man's place to venture into the heavens. At the time, he had credited the idea to wackos; at this point he was not so sure. Now that the smoke had cleared and a little time had passed, his mind reeled.

When Lucifer dropped by to discuss the new, updated version of *The Guide*, Dirk showed him the damage.

"Did you lose the new entries?"

"That's not the point. I think I need protection, maybe even round-the-clock security."

"Well," Lucifer began, spreading his hands in an expansive motion that indicated denial, "I can see you need a new desk and computer. That will be no problem. In fact, I can guarantee this won't happen again, because your new system won't be tied into the Internet at all. You will be directly connected to the Outernet." Lucifer smiled

"The Outernet?"

"The Internet is for those inside a corporal body. The Outernet is for those not limited by such confines," Lucifer explained.

Dirk grinned. "I've gotten so far outside the box I'm non-corporeal!"

"As for security, I don't really see how I can do much better for you than you have for yourself. You have both your feline sister and your guardian angel living here. As you know, I am very short-staffed …

"It's not that I'm complaining, exactly," Lucifer whined, pulling a small silver file out of his waistcoat and absentmindedly buffing his nails, "but, as you've already seen, God has a lot more help. Look at the vast number of people who believe he's three. Right there, that cuts his workload into thirds. Then there's the virgin—"

"The Virgin? Mary? What's the Virgin Mary like?"

"Let me put it this way. How'd you like your claim to fame to be as a virgin? And not just *a* virgin, but *the* Virgin. Talk about frustration!" The Devil tossed a lock of glossy black hair from his forehead, white teeth flashing. "That's one tense lady, lemme tell you."

"Well," Dirk sighed, "except for the houris, I have no virgin experience. In fact, I have two females in my life, and they don't get along. How do sultans and Mormons do it?"

Apparently, even the Devil could not answer this question, for with a hasty good-bye, Lucifer gathered up the new manuscript and departed.

Dirk had to run a few errands. He needed typing paper. Mary needed catnip. Angelica needed French ticklers.

The stationery/cat drugs/sex toys mall lot was full. Cursing silently but thoroughly, he risked parked in a red zone.

The risk was a bad one, though not primarily for him. Neatly wired under the hood of his car was a bomb, timed to explode when Dirk started the engine. But due, once again, to supernatural interference, the bomb exploded when the car was placidly parked in the tow-away zone. Dirk's only consolation was that it took the policeman, who was writing Dirk a rather expensive ticket, with it.

Dirk briefly considered borrowing the cop's motorcycle but decided in favor of a cab. After all, although Lucifer balked at providing security, he had an apparently bottomless expense account.

Rapture Born Again

*After coming into contact with a religious man I always feel
I must wash my hands.* —Friedrich Nietzsche

On the way home, Dirk had the cab stop by a mini-market.
Dirk dashed from the cab to buy some beer and cigarettes.
Having his car blow up had unnerved him. In a situation like this, French
ticklers, paper, and nip were not enough. The cigarettes were inside a
vending machine which pictured Santa in his snow suit, sharing a Coca-
Cola with a blond in a swim suit.

Judging from its long slots, this behemoth ate only bills.

Sighing, Dirk pulled out a crumpled dollar bill. Smoothing it
between his hands, he attempted to force-feed the cigarette machine.
As he'd expected, although the machine made a number of groans and
squeaks, it resolutely refused to accept the wrinkled dollar. As quickly as
Dirk tried to force the bill in, the machine spit it out.

They ought to have a steamer, for ironing bills.

Finally, he trotted up to the counter, exchanging his battered bills for
new starched ones.

Returning to the machine, he fed the dollar into the slot. This time
the machine ate it with alacrity; in fact, it was so delighted with the
starched bill that it continued sucking long after the dollar had disappeared. Before Dirk could protest, or even drop his beer, he was sucked
into darkness.

He awoke smelling of beer, still clasping a flattened can in one
hand.

Above him towered golden gates bearing the inscription, LET JESUS
TAKE THE WORRY OUT OF BEING DEAD.

DIRK QUIGBY'S GUIDE
TO THE BORN AGAIN AFTERLIFE

Note: "Born Again Manor" is a new suburb with rentals available.

END DESTINATION:

Heaven with Jesus or Hell with Satan.

ENTRY REQUIREMENTS:

Why be born again? Man (and woman doubly so) is born with an evil heart. *As a special one-time salvation offer from Jesus,* God will give you a first-class heart, packed in a brand-new body.

Believe that Jesus died for your sins.

Say it. Confess!

Confess in public.

Confess loudly

Confess with tears.

If you have hate in your heart, let it flow. God hates fags, Jews, and agnostics. This is the only true church of Jesus Christ.

QUALITY RATINGS:

Perks: ★ —Avoid a lot of really unpleasant stuff that is going to ensue after the Rapture. The Rapture takes place when Jesus secretly returns to Earth and transports true believers up Heaven. Dead body parts and individual molecules from two millenniums-worth of dead Christians will be reconstituted into their original bodies, then converted into spirits. *Surely, it would be easier to make them spirits to begin with? That God guy can be such a show off!* They will rise out of their graves and ascend to meet Jesus.

This will be followed by a second mass migration of living Born-

Agains. These will levitate into the air, passing through ceilings, cars, roofs, etc. to meet Jesus in the sky.

Families will be eating dinner, when suddenly Billy-Ray will rise from his seat, *grasping for a last pork rind*, pass through the roof, and keep ascending through the air. *Now that will be something to see.*

The vast majority of humans, nasty nonbelievers all, will be left to deal with the numerous planes, trains, and automobiles crashing all around them. *I asked one of the faithful if, in case of rapture, I could have his car, since a religious fanatic had blown up mine. But, though he had five pick-ups in his front yard, they all lacked either wheels or engines.*

When the Rapture comes, those left behind will endure seven years of tribulation, inflicted on the world by the Antichrist, disguised as leader of a one-world government. But some of those shocked by the sudden disappearance of their loved ones will become true Bible-believing Christians who will band together to resist the wiles of the Antichrist. They will conduct secret evangelistic campaigns to grow the power and numbers of their "tribulation force."

Finally, after seven years of dirty, filthy, rotten Antichrist rule, Jesus will return. He will defeat the army of evil at Armageddon (a large plain in Israel). *Declaring "the era of big Antichrist government over,"* He will take command, and reign for one thousand years over a "politically reconstituted kingdom of Israel" *just add water*. The Jews will finally see the error of their ways (*about time*) and convert to Christianity.

The basis for belief in the Rapture lies in the Bible, specifically Thessalonians 4:16 *and Fallacies 6:66:*

"For the Lord himself shall descend from heaven with a shout ... *Hey dead people, come here!* ... the dead in Christ shall rise first: Then we which are alive ... shall be caught up together with them."

If you've always wanted to fly but are too lazy to get a pilot's license, you'll love this place.

Music: ★ —Loud, off-key, fervent and annoying.

Food: ★ —If you like grease, lard, fried or pickled unidentifiable animal guts, and deep fried Oreos, you'll love it. Oreos are coated in eggs and pancake batter before being deep, deep-fried, then rolled in powdered sugar. Eat enough and you're guaranteed a quick trip to the afterlife.

Drink: ★ —Technically just water and juice, but Nyquil is very popular.

Accommodations: ★★★ —A mansion in the sky with plastic flowers, encircled by the flames of hell. Here you can actually see and hear all those once-borns squirming and squealing in agony.

Entry Requirements: ★★

OVERALL RATING: ★

When Dirk returned, Angelica was waiting. She looked up at Dirk in obvious annoyance.

"Where have you been? And—what are those?" She pointed long elegant fingers at an unseemly array of brightly colored buttons that decorated Dirk's sweater in a haphazard manner.

Dirk glanced down: "I love Jesus," "The wages of sin is Death," "1 cross + 4 nails = 4 given," "America needs a faith lift," and "Are you as close to Jesus as you are to my shirt?"

Dirk shrugged, he was hungry. He had not partaken of the fried buffalo wings or pickled pig's trotters. Now he desired nothing more than a cold beer and a meal that had not been breaded, fried, or soaked in brine.

"'Prevent Truth Decay, Read the Bible!'" Angelica read. "Where were you?"

"Some god-awful Born-Again suburb," Dirk groaned. "These Born-Again developments seem to be popping up everywhere, just like fleas."

"'God Said It, I Believe It, That Settles It,'" Angelica read.

"All have a vehement hatred of other beliefs," Dirk complained. "They are more intent on disparaging the damned—everyone except themselves—than praising the blessed or blessing the praiseworthy. If I were certain of getting into Heaven, I would pity, not despise, the condemned. After all, isn't being consigned to hell enough?"

"'God Hates Fags,'" Angelica read. "Humm, even I cannot claim such insight into our creator's preferences."

"Tonight I was dragged into a reserve of Southern Born-Again Baptists from Oklahoma.

"What can you say about a state whose motto is: 'We're O.K.!' How about: 'We aren't really awful!' Or 'We don't completely suck!' I guess that's too big to put on a license plate, though. There is also that most popular of ditties, 'You're doing fine Oklahoma.' 'You're doing fine'... not excellent or even good ...? Not the most ambitious state in the nation! The eleventh commandment, 'Ye shall plant pickups in your garden and they shall multiply.' Communion consists of unidentifiable pig parts and deep fried Oreos."

"'Jesus is God, with Skin on,'" Angelica laughed. "'WORRY. God Knows All About You.'"

"Does he?" Dirk opened his eyes wide in mock horror; he leaned over and kissed her.

"'Lead Me Not Into Temptation—I Know My Way,'" Angelica read huskily. "They certainly do like their buttons." She slowly removed "God is Groovy" and "Burn like Nero" from his breast pocket.

"They're made in Salt Lake City," Dirk murmured. Nuzzling her neck, he inhaled deeply.

"Salt Lake City?" Angelica moaned. "I didn't think either Born-

Agains or Baptists were fond of Mormons."

"The Mormons," Dirk began, slowly unbuttoning the top button of her blouse, "have a Colorado post box." He unbuttoned the second button. "If the Born-Agains knew the source of their icons," he bent down and gently kissed the tops of her breasts, "was the Devil's cult …" Dirk cupped his hand around each breast and lifted them free of her blouse. Angelica groaned. "… They'd burn the existing inventory," he murmured while circling each nipple with his tongue.

"Mormons," Angelica panted, working her hands inside his shirt, "work in devious ways their religious artifacts to sell." She began to circumnavigate the circumference of his pants.

"To be fair," Dirk whispered, "Mormons aren't exactly noted for their open-minded embracing of other faiths either."

"No," Angelica breathed her agreement. "They aren't noted for their Catholic tastes, but then, neither are Catholics."

She reached into his pants, thus effectively ending further philosophizing.

Whirled Peas

Sacred cows make the best hamburger.
—Mark Twain

Notes:
"Rapture Ready" is the second most popular Web site on the Internet. Another popular site is www.godhatesfags.com.

Dirk had decided to make a spare hard copy of the guide. Although he was now connected to the Outernet and unlikely to have any worldly interference with his computer, bombs had been going off, or rather not going off, with alarming frequency. Besides, he was out of cigarettes.

With his *Afterlife* securely stowed in a carton inside his backpack, Dirk jumped on his bike and pedaled toward a nearby copy shop. Nowadays Dirk traveled by bicycle or taxi. Even before his car had exploded, his frequent disappearances into different dimensions had made finding a parking space tricky.

Arriving at the copy shop, Dirk locked his bike to a post and went inside.

At the front of the store was a counter, where customers waited for their turn to be insulted and hassled by the surly staff. One of the clerks was a muscular, murderous-looking bald fellow. Tattooed snakes encircled his biceps and they undulated with every movement. The clerk's co-worker was a hard-faced Mexican girl with a Dunn-Edwards facial. She was popping her gum in a decidedly non-service-oriented manner.

In the back were four self-service machines eager to reproduce. The machines had been known to eat manuscripts, but Dirk decided to risk it. The machine displayed a bewildering array of buttons, as well as a tiny, confusing diagram of how to insert paper. Ten tries and seven dollars later, Dirk had it down. The trick was to divide the book into five-page sections and feed them slowly into the copier while softly humming a soothing ditty about the joys of duplication.

He had managed to copy about half the manuscript, when he felt a pain in his shoulder. Turning around, he saw that the muscle-bound snake man was behind him, a malevolent look on his normally malevolent face.

"Ain't you that Anti-Christ Dirk Quigby?"

Fortunately, Dirk's left hand was still feeding papers into the slot, and fortunately the machine, which had apparently taken a shine to Dirk, chose this moment to suck him into the feeder. The last things Dirk saw, before he was flattened into the next afterlife, were the frightened, baffled eyes of the serpent-enhanced behemoth.

When Dirk awoke, he was lying in a heap on top of some ink-black clouds. He was in front of an enormous obsidian gate. *"The blacker the skin, the quicker you're in; the whiter the flesh, suffer, die, rot in death"* was emblazoned upon the gate in shining onyx letters of a darker shade of black.

DIRK QUIGBY'S GUIDE TO THE NATION OF ISLAM AFTERLIFE

Note: We're talking extreme affirmative action.

At first, I was surprised to be asked to chronicle the Nation of Islam afterlife, assuming that it was merely a suburb of Islam *though I never mind visiting that garden paradise.* However, my view was incorrect. Although Nation of Islamers (henceforth referred to as NOIs) do *sort of* follow the "five pillars of faith": pray five times daily, fast during Ramadan, etc., there the resemblance ends. The mission of the Nation of Islam is to resurrect the spiritual, mental, social, and economic condition of black men and women.

In 1930, door-to-door salesman Wali Fard Muhammad found the lost Nation of Islam in Detroit *where it had been hiding.* W.F. Muhammad spent three years there, teaching his personal version of Islam to a disciple named Elijah Poole. *Step one: convert name to Muhammad.*

In 1934, W.F. Muhammad also disappeared, and the Honorable Elijah Muhammad assumed leadership of NOI. The Honorable Elijah Muhammad, *in obedience to the creed of chastity and moderation,* fathered thirteen children with several of his secretaries, traveled in a private jet, and wore an $150,000 jewel-studded fez. *After all, if you're a prophet, you got to dress like one.*

When Elijah died his son, Warith Deen Muhammad, took over. W.D. Muhammad was a rebel; he changed his name to Mohammed! He disbanded the Fruit of Islam (a Black Muslim militia), *converting it into a peaceful garment company called the Fruit of Islam's Loom.* He revealed that his Dad was not really a God. And that all whites were not blue-eyed devils; *some were green- or brown-eyed imps.*

In 1981, Louis Farrakhan reformed the "Nation of Islam." After all, W.D. Muhammad was turning NOI into just another whitey-loving Sunni Islam group.

END DESTINATION:

To my vast disappointment, there were no houris. For one thing, houris are too white. For another, NOI's concern is with the here, not the hereafter. They concentrate on the psychological resurrection of mentally dead black people.

You must realize that the universe was created seventy-eight trillion years ago. Eventually the atoms of life, *which were putting in long hours and working overtime,* produced brains. The brains, *which were having trouble moving around,* created God. The first God was black (as are all successive Gods). Gods usually live about a hundred or two hundred years, although there is a record of one really old God who lived to be a thousand years old. *This record is on display next to the lost half of the Bible, the whole of stolen black culture, the Golden tablets, and the Holy Grail in the Lost Artifacts of God Museum.* Every twenty-five thousand years a successive BLACK god creates a new civilization.

The Shabazz were the first humans. They came to Earth sixty-six trillion years ago and were black. The black man is the true seed of Abraham. From him came all brown, yellow, red, and black people. The Shabazz lived an advanced and righteous life. But six thousand years ago, Paradise was lost. An evil genius, Mr. Yakub (also known as "the big head scientist") began a genetic breeding program to create white people. When the Shabazz realized what he was up to, they marooned him on an island in the Aegean Sea. This, however, did not stop evil Mr. Yakub. Within six hundred years, using a special method of birth control *called rhythm,* he had produced white humans. Caucasians (also referred to as "blue-eyed devils") are inherently evil as well as genetically inferior. It isn't their fault; they just haven't evolved yet. But for some unspecified reason, they were allowed to dominate and rule the world for six thousand years. That reign ended in 1914, though, for another unspecified reason, a seventy-year period of grace extended it to 1984. W.D. Fard came (from Detroit) to show blacks how to reclaim the world, a goal they would definitely accomplish by the year 2000.

You must also realize that Jesus was a human prophet, born from an adulterous relationship between Mary and Joseph. Joseph was already married. Mary was just a fling. No surprise, all whites are evil, but Jews are the worst.

Jesus was stabbed in the heart by a policeman (*probably a Jewish one ... Maybe that jerk who gave Mel Gibson a ticket!*).

The universe is currently ruled by a council of twenty-four black scientists, managed by a head scientist known as Allah. And Wali Fard, the Honorable *Prolific* Elijah Muhammad, and Louis Farrakhan, are Gods.

Though Fard disappeared in 1933, he is alive on the Mother Wheel. The Mother Wheel is a circular plane made in Japan, a very, very long time ago. It cost fifteen billion dollars in gold, *back then that was real money!* It's constructed from steel of a toughness as yet undiscovered in America. It travels thousands of miles per hour ... The Mother Wheel (half mile by a half mile) contains 1,500 smaller wheels. Each carries three bombs. These bombs created Earth's mountains. *Who said the mountain can't come to Muhammad?* The idiot white men imagine the Mother Wheels to be UFOs, spying on military operations. They pretend these planes are fiction, but they are real. The Mother Wheel can crumble buildings with a sound.

W. Fard is not alone on the Mother Wheel; The Eternal Honorable Elijah Muhammad is there to keep him company. Elijah Muhammad is not dead. He "escaped a death plot, was restored to health, and is at this very moment aboard that huge wheel-like plane flying over our heads," *having a wonderful time.*

Caucasian Muslims are brothers in the faith of Islam and should be honored as such. Unfortunately, being inferior and evil, they are not accepted into the NOI. All other races are eligible, *though not exactly welcome.*

QUALITY RATINGS:

Perks: *Let me get back to you on that.*

Music: ★★ —There were a lot of spirituals, but rap seems pretty popular these days.

Food: ★★★ —Organic and grainy. Lots of baked goods. Dark food is popular here.

Drink: ★ —No alcohol, but hot chocolate is a crowd-pleaser because it's almost black.

Accommodations: ★★ —Clean, modest and hut-like ... unless you are a Prophet.

Entry Requirements: ★ —Totally dependent on your color

OVERALL RATING: ★

Dirk returned to his couch confused and tired, he smoked a cigarette and pondered the amazing effect that melanin had had on the human spirit and the spiritual human. Who would have *imagined that a little pigment would have had such reverberating repercussions?*

Jews never called each other "kike." Hispanics never called each other "spick," so why did blacks call each other "nigger"?

Why was it okay to say, "people of color" but not "colored people"?

Dirk brushed his white teeth and went to bed.

God's Embrace

I believe there is something out there watching over us.
Unfortunately, it's the government. —Woody Allen

Dirk exited the grocery store after trying to decide whether Mary would prefer tuna, salmon, or chicken. In the end, he bought all three.

He had only gone a few steps when a large, hairy man ran toward him shouting, "God is great." The man was wearing a Bill Blass vest, fashionably hung with dynamite.

Before he could embrace Dirk however, Angelica emerged seemingly out of nowhere, but actually out of the 99-cent store where she'd been shopping for nail polish. Miracles are so often easily explained.

She inserted herself between Dirk and his admirer. The last thing Dirk remembered seeing was a pair of exceptionally hairy eyebrows suspended in space. He awoke to find Angelica looking ravishing, if not ravenous.

The Sun and the Moon

*Adam blamed Eve, Eve blamed the serpent, and the serpent
didn't have a leg to stand on.* —Anonymous

Mary had brought home a little pink Barbie Doll brush, which she
carried around in her mouth. She adored having her whiskers
combed with it.

"You're such a girlie cat," Dirk laughed. "Where do you suppose
she got it? Do you think she went out and mugged a Barbie last night?
Are we going to get a knock on the door from an irate Ken or G.I. Joe
demanding restitution?"

Angelica didn't reply. She looked down at her hands, minutely exam-
ining her latest nail extravaganza. From between the corners of her closed
mouth, the delicate white tips of canines were clearly visible.

Dirk decided it was a good time to do the wash.

Some of his clothes were permanently stained.

These journeys to the afterlife are hell on a man's wardrobe.

Why the Devil can't—

Before Dirk could even finish his thought, he was sucked into the
dryer. He awoke some time later, after the completion of the spin cycle,
dry and slightly linty.

Iron gates enclosed a brick-red temple topped with blue shingles and
tilting eaves. Inscribed on the archway were Asian characters. It was the
Holy Spirit Association for the Unification of World Christianity. The
devotees are called "Moonies," but not to their face.

Sun Myung Moon was born Presbyterian, but that changed in 1935. Sun Myung was sixteen, which is more like fifteen, because Koreans view the prenatal nine months as year one. (They also gain a year on the Korean New Year, which is lunar and varies. This is why Koreans live longer than Westerners.) *Anyway, Moon was on a camping trip, praying in the mountains, when he ran into Jesus.*

"I'm a failure!" Jesus said. "I was born without original sin. Dad expected me to marry and produce a planetful of sinless children. Instead, I got crucified!" The Trinity was intended to be Jesus, His wife, and God.

The Jews really fucked up when they murdered Jesus.

God had sulked for a bit, but now He was ready to take action. *Jesus, for His part, was rather annoyed God hadn't acted a bit sooner … say, prior to the nails.*

Jesus begged Moon to establish the only true church of Jesus Christ, but vanished before providing directions. So Moon improvised. He penned *The Divine Principle*, explaining that God created the universe to manifest true love. *He messed up a little when he formulated the food chain.*

End Destination:

Go to the spirit world. If you eat junk food, have sex out of wedlock, or are not a Unificationist, go to spirit Hell. (Also, no smoking, drink, or drugs.)

However, you can get to Heaven posthumously by becoming a Unificationist and converting all your fellow ghouls. In the end, everyone will be saved … even Satan.

ENTRY REQUIREMENTS:

God is perfectly harmonious with positive (male) and negative (female) aspects. The Holy Spirit is feminine energy from God. But the universe got off track early on.

Adam and Eve were meant to be the True Parents. They had plans for a *June* wedding, but Eve met Lucifer *wearing an outfit of genuine snakeskin, and Eve ended up with a snake in the oven. Lucifer denies this, although he carries a picture of Eve in his wallet.*

Then Eve seduced Adam. In excitement he exploded before entry. *In his defense, it was the first time in human history anyone had been laid.* Thus, Cain, and Abel were spawn of Eve and Lucifer.

Cain inherited some nasty serpentine genes: he murdered his brother Abel, and passed his "false love" down through the genera-tions. *Apparently, "false love" is a dominant trait.*

Cain, Lucifer, Jews, and Communists are Evil. Able, God, Unifica-tionists, and Democracy are good.

Reverend Moon and his second wife, Hak Ja Han, are the True Parents. *Haile Selassie's press agent was better.* And only those matched and married by the True Parents can enter Heaven. Even Jesus was ineligible until Reverend Moon posthumously married him to a nice Korean girl.

The offspring of the True Parents are sinless. One was arrested for wife beating and cocaine and another committed suicide. Heung Jin Moon, Moon's second son died in a car crash at seventeen. He, the "king of the spirits" (ranking higher than Jesus), is currently giving seminars in heaven for famous ghouls.

Reverend Moon marries couples from varied backgrounds to unify the human race. *He obviously hasn't seen some of the marriages I have!* Unificationists must remain celibate until married by Moon, then produce herds of children.

The *Blessing,* or mass wedding ceremony, is the most important ritual. Imbibe Holy Wine, which has more secret ingredients than Coca-Cola. It contains actual blood from Reverend Moon and Hak Ja Han. Swallow it and your blood transforms from Lucifer's into God's. *Talk about transubstantiation!* There are reserves of Moon's blood in cold storage so Holy Wine production will not be affected by his death.

After a Unificationist wedding comes the Indemnity Ceremony, where the Devil is beaten out of the body. Couples are given a stickball bat. The husband beats the wife three times on the buttocks as hard as he can. Then *if she is still conscious* the wife beats the husband.

There's a three-day post wedding ceremony to prepare the newlyweds for sex. The first two nights, the woman is on top, symbolizing "Eve's Sin." On the third night and forever after, the man is on top, symbolizing Adam's dominance. *I couldn't find any information on blowjobs.*

Only those matched and married by the Parents can produce children born without nasty snake genes. Women married to non-Unification members must be remarried to stop the spread of said genes.

In Moon's early days he practiced *Pi Ka Rum* (cleansing of the womb). Reverend Moon purified wombs by having sex with a woman. She in turn would have sex with her husband and other married men to spread the Messiah's blood. If you are a man, achieve purification by donating your bank account to the Church.

Eventually the world will be composed of sinless beings ruled by the Parents. Korean will become the world language, and the world will be paradise. *Although it will have a weird verb structure.*

One way to get God's blessing is by enduring mistreatment. Rev. Moon suffered, spending thirteen months in prison for tax evasion and conspiracy to obstruct justice—even though he was endorsed by thirty-six U.S. presidents, from George Washington to Richard Nixon, during a spirit world conference.

"People of America ..." Jefferson said, "... Follow the teachings of Rev. Sun Myung Moon, the Messiah to all people." Madison was equally enthusiastic. The event was chaired by Dwight D. Eisenhower. Franklin D. Roosevelt offered the closing prayer.

In spite of the fact that communism is of Satan and capitalism is of God, many Unificationists go out in groups to sell flowers, what-nots, and widgets to build the coffers of the Church. *This single-party control of whatnots and widgets, and the division of profits (usually in the form of a watery vegetarian dinners) seemed suspiciously reminiscent of Communism to me.*

However, Moonies' politics are very conservative. Their news-paper, the *Washington Times*, prints rightwing ideology as news.

QUALITY RATINGS:
Perks: ½★ —This is a great place:
    If you're married and want a divorce.
    Have always wanted to learn Korean.
    Don't like balancing your checkbook.
    Enjoy a bit of S and M.
Music: ★ —The Koreans claim to have invented drums. When they aren't drumming, they use a scale that reminded me of catgut played while attached to the cat.
Food: ★ ★ ★ —Like kim chee?
Drink: ★ —If you're into vampires, you'll like the Holy Wine.
Accommodations: ★ ★ —Clean and simple. If you're prone to

backaches, you may not like sitting on pillows at the table or sleeping on a mattress on the floor.

Entry Requirements: ★
OVERALL RATING: ★

Dirk returned to his homing couch half an hour or three days later, but it had seemed longer. Dirk had not been crazy about ejaculating snakes and holy marriages. He knew that the time variations between Heaven and Earth had to do with relativity. If a place was undesirable he was gone longer, but he could never predict the variance.

The only constants were that departure was always unpredictable, unpleasant, and unnatural. No matter how often it happened, Dirk could not get used to being sucked, yanked, or wrenched into other worlds.

God Spelled Backward

There may be more than one way to skin a cat,
but you only get one try per cat. —Anonymous

Mary fattened up nicely on her new diet of tuna, chicken, and other carnivorous delicacies. The time (albeit brief) not spent in napping, gazing at invisible objects, ingesting massive amounts of catnip and eating, she employed by rubbing against Dirk's legs, jumping into his lap, and sleeping beside him when Angelica was not around. It bugged the hell out of Angelica.

But one afternoon, Angelica brought home a Doberman. "I don't see why I can't have a pet too," she pouted. "I need to lavish my affections on something while you play with that cat."

"She's not a pet. She's my sister!"

"Well, maybe John-John's my brother,"

"John-John?"

"I've always liked the Kennedys."

"The Kennedys," Dirk scoffed. "What is it with them? Everyone in that family is named John, Robert, or Caroline. Oh, they try and disguise it occasionally by calling themselves 'Jack,' 'Bobbie,' or 'John-John'... but it won't wash! What is it? Bobbie Jr.? Bobbie Jr. the III? Shit! They even marry Carolines, and when they don't they marry a Caroline, they marry a Jackie!"

Angelica looked sulky and scratched John-John behind the ears.

"I don't believe you have a Doberman for a brother," Dirk concluded.

Angelica shrugged.

"I don't believe he's your brother and I don't want him living here."

"Well," Angelica mused, "you could get rid of Mary, and I can find a good home for my little angel. Couldn't I, baby?" she cooed at John-John.

"She's my sister!" Dirk expostulated.

"I'm not at all sure about that," Angelica replied. "And even if she is, it's not as if sibling love were a natural thing. In fact, if I'm not mistaken, sibling rivalry is much more common than sibling love. Many species destroy their siblings, you know; pelicans always push the youngest, smallest chick out of the nest. Sand sharks eat their younger siblings in utero."

"I'm not a sand shark."

"No, you'd have much better teeth if you were."

Dirk remained silent, gritting his imperfect teeth.

"Well," he finally said, "I, for one, was under the misconception that angels were ... well, angelic. I also believe that in most cases of cannibalism, it's the predatory female who eats her mate. Perhaps loving an angel is more akin to loving a praying mantis than ... well ... than an angel," he finished lamely.

"Males!" Angelica scoffed. "Did you know that the Hawaiian monk seal is almost extinct?"

"What?" Dirk was having difficulty understanding the connection.

"What do you think is making them extinct?"

Dirk looked blank, "It's just another of those myriad of things I don't know, I suppose."

"Yes. Well, as usual males are the problem. They are so eager for sexual fulfillment, that they mob the females, usually killing them in the process. Your species is attempting to save them by injecting males with drugs that suppress their rather overactive libido. Some species are better left alone, I say. Even God had a few off moments. Anyway, it's odd to worry about monk seals when you are killing off so many other species so very quickly—monk seals?" Angelica snorted. "Whoever named them monk seals? I ask you."

"Are you finished?" Dirk inquired. "I know we aren't the greatest species in this or any world. Please accept my apologies on behalf of my kind." Dirk tried to sound hard and flat, but his voice cracked with misery.

Angelica looked at him as if she hadn't seen him for a long, long time.

"Oh my poor, poor darling," she suddenly cooed, holding out her arms.

Without volition, Dirk fell into them.

Make-up sex was great!

John-John became part of the family.

Mary, contrary to expectation, liked him just fine. She, Dirk, and John-John became a rather happy trio.

Angelica was not pleased.

Moreover, she was feeling thwarted that there had been no fresh electrical attempts on Dirk's life. Like an amphetamine addict craving her next high, Angelica was craving voltage.

Doubtless this was the reason that Dirk, returning home one evening, found her hungrily chewing an extension cord. She took to blow-drying her hair in the bathtub and toasting bread in the shower. When she began vacuuming the neighbor's pool, he decided things had gone far enough.

Dirk called Lucifer.

"Power junkies," Lucifer commiserated, "one sees it so much these days. God had no idea there'd be so much raw energy."

"What do you mean?" Dirk asked, lighting a cigarette.

Lucifer contemplated his perfect nails and removed his small silver file from his waistcoat. Distractedly he began to buff.

"As you know, God put a tiny bit of energy inside each of His creations. This enables their guardian angels to monitor them. In order to encourage monitoring, God made energy very—uh—pleasant to angels, in much the same way He made sex pleasant to humans. It encourages His desired behavior."

"God wants us to have sex?" Dirk, who was feeling a bit confused, asked. "Most Heavens seem to view sex as just about the worst, nastiest thing you could do."

"Don't you remember that bit about 'Go forth and multiply'?" Lucifer inquired, unconsciously stroking his newly filed nails with his thumb. "He wasn't talking about math, you know. It's a human concept that sex is bad. If things had gone *my* way, you guys could all be guiltlessly humping away like rabbits."

"But what about Angelica?"

"Ah, Angelica …Well, like all small-time angels, she is used to a very minor intake of energy. Now she's suddenly getting bomb after bomb. It's like taking a guy who drinks a cup of instant coffee and putting him on a diet of cocaine. She wants more.

"When God in His infinite wisdom made energy so very … pleasant to angels, he didn't really foresee cars, bombs, radios, iPods, vacuum cleaners, and the Internet … All those widgets just waiting for an angel."

"So?" Dirk prompted.

"Soooo," Lucifer continued drawing out the word with evident relish. "Some angels can hold their energy and some can't. They were created in a simpler time. When exposed to all that power they have no control. They go crazy."

"What about computer crashes, or the space shuttle explosion?"

"What about them?"

"Were they caused by addicted angels?"

Lucifer stared absently at his fingers. "I really couldn't say. But I can tell you one thing: your species is really a lot better at constructing perfectly functioning devices than you have been led to believe." He glanced piercingly up at Dirk, flashing an impish grin.

Alien Abduction

A casual stroll through the lunatic asylum shows that faith does not prove anything. —Friedrich Nietzsche

Dirk, Angelica, and John-John had gone to the beach.

It's a pity, Dirk thought, *that Mary can't join us.* However, he was wise enough not to say that aloud. Not that he was sure it mattered; Angelica seemed perfectly capable of reading his mind. Still, if he said something aloud, she could not ignore it and it was almost certain to cause a quarrel. Angelica had not even been particularly pleased to include John-John on their outing.

"Dealing with one odd species is enough," she'd grumbled. But John-John had looked so crestfallen that the males prevailed.

Dirk and Angelica strolled slowly arm-in-arm down the beach, while John-John frolicked in the waves. Occasionally Dirk would pick up a piece of driftwood and toss it far down the beach. John-John was in ecstasy. Dirk glowed with contentment. Times like these had been rare lately. Often Angelica was gone, whether on a mission from God or on a quest for fresh electricity, Dirk could not be sure. He hoped the former and feared the latter. Now, however, in the brisk sea breeze Angelica seemed at ease, more like her old self, the morning's contention forgotten.

John-John raced up, clenching a wet stick. Dirk tried to retrieve it, but the dog wrestled, dancing from side to side and playfully growling. When Dirk let go his hands were black and sticky with tar.

"Got to wash my hands," said Dirk, bending to kiss Angelica. "Save my place?"

He entered the restroom and scrubbed. The tar was stubborn. He gave up while his hands were still slightly tacky and brown. He pressed the button on the hand dryer, vigorously rubbing his hands together. Not noticing any drying effect, he pulled his hands away. The dryer pulled back.

Dirk was sucked upward. He awoke surrounded by stars. Movie stars.

Dirk Quigby's Guide
to the Scientologist Afterlife

Note: Lucifer said he had to pull out all the stops to get me into this Heaven. The "Operating Thetan" (OTs) of this establishment were adamant I attend some very pricy assist sessions with an "e-meter" before entering. Luckily, the Devil has an apparently bottomless expense account, and provided material assurance that our motives were spiritual.

In 1954, science fiction writer L. Ron Hubbard received divine inspiration: "The way to make a million dollars is to start a religion." Thus was the Church of Scientology founded.

End Destination:

You are already a spirit that can achieve anything; you merely need to be freed from present and past-life traumas, false memories, and implanted beliefs. The only way to do this is through the Church of Scientology. You too can become superhuman merely by expunging past traumas and savings accounts.

In Scientology there is no afterlife, death, Heaven, or Hell. Eventually, after spending all your pocket money on auditing sessions, you will become an Operating Thetan, like Tom Cruise and John Travolta. Operating Thetans can control Matter, Energy, Space, and Time *and sometimes even a movie critic.*

Once we were all happy thetans, immortal spirits, who created earth as a plaything. But today we are not godlike, perfect beings, and that's because trillions and trillions of years ago, some nasty aliens messed with our psyches.

Seventy-five million years ago, Xenu, an exceptionally evil alien, destroyed multitudes of thetans.

Xenu ruled a Galactic Confederacy consisting of twenty-six stars and seventy-six planets, including Earth (known as Teegeeack). The planets were horribly overpopulated, each containing about 178 billion people.

Xenu, with the assistance of renegades and psychiatrists, paralyzed billions of people with injections of alcohol and glycol, under the pretense that they were going to receive income tax audits.

The frozen people were loaded into space planes and brought to Teegeeack. They were placed near volcanoes and exploded with H-bombs. This is the reason that *Dianetics* (the fundamental Scientology book) pictures a volcano on its cover. L Ron Hubbard knew we'd be drawn to it by atavistic memories. The disembodied souls exploded into the air, where they were captured by an electronic ribbon and sucked into vacuum zones around the world.

Afterward the hundreds of billions of paralyzed, exploded thetans were forced to watch 3-D super-colossal motion pictures for thirty-six days *with no popcorn*. This brainwashed them into believing all kinds of wild ideas, like the existence of God, the Devil, etc. The blown-up, movied-out thetans were then transported to Hawaii and Las Palmas for packaging.

In addition to implanting beliefs in the thetans, the brainwashing deprived them of their identity. They lost the ability to differentiate between each other, and clustered together in groups of thousands. Each cluster of thetans clamored into the few remaining bodies that survived the explosion. These became known as Body Thetans (BTs), because they lack bodies. They are still clinging to, and adversely affecting each and every one of us, except Scientologists who have passed OT III.

Officers loyal to the thetans waged a six-year campaign against Xenu, ultimately capturing and imprisoning him in an electronic mountain trap, where he remains to this day.

This is "space opera." Anyone learning this before he is ready might die!

Before receiving knowledge of Xenu, OT III's must sign a waiver promising never to tell what they are about to learn. Then they are handed a manila envelope containing the secret. *No wonder they appear so calm during the Academy Awards.*

Before you can remove BTs from your body, you must destroy your reactive mind, becoming a clear.

To get clear, an auditor (who would be like a therapist, except that therapy is horribly evil) will wire you to an electropsychometer, or e-meter. Answering questions while clasping two electrodes in your hands will show where you are blocked. Thus you can find and destroy implants and engrams. Implants are false memories; engrams are the result of negative experiences or pain. When you are clear, the needle will balance, or "float." Only then can you begin removing the hundreds of thousands of Body Thetans that are clinging to you.

Each Body Thetan in a cluster is a full-fledged thetan. Each responds to normal auditing procedure. Clusters must be disassembled one thetan at a time. *Very expensive.* Once a BT has been freed from a cluster, it wanders off to start an independent existence as an ordinary thetan with its own soul *and pocket money.* All blocks must be removed before you become an OT.

Scientology is completely scientific, NOT LIKE PSYCHO-THERAPY, which is evil twaddle. Scientologists abhor psychotherapy, Freud, and psychiatry more than vegans despise McDonald's. Psychiatrists are an ancient evil, responsible for Xenu's genocide, World War I, pain, sex, and the Bank of England. They are behind a worldwide conspiracy to attack Scientology and create a world government run by psychiatrists on behalf of Soviet Russia.

Sickness and pain are all in your head. They don't exist. If you are injured, simply go the place where you were hurt and press against it. *This can be challenging if the injury involves a speeding car.*

A fever is cured by holding something very still and getting the fever to flow into that object. *This leads to loads of burned-out widgets.*

A mother must deliver her baby in silence so that the child isn't polluted by any nasty pain engrams.

Children are just tiny adults. Schools use a device called a learning accelerator, similar to the e-meter.

Limit contact with wogs—people outside Scientology, or as Hubbard defined them, "common, ordinary, run-of-the-mill, garden-variety humanoids."

The highest level of training takes place on *The Freewinds*, a cruise ship. Perhaps this is because L. Ron Hubbard was forced to spend many earthly years on a boat in international waters due to some nasty implants beamed into the minds of IRS auditors.

In 1986, Hubbard deliberately discarded his body to conduct research in spirit form. He is now living "on a planet a galaxy away."

QUALITY RATINGS:
Perks: ★ ★ ★ ★ —An Operating Thetan, who has been cleared of

Body Thetans *and his bank account,* can control Matter, Energy, Space, Time, *and never has a bad-hair day.*

The OT perceives its body to be transparent, since there are no BTs attached to it. (*An OT never eats BLTs.*)

Once an OT, you will have a perfect memory, perfect vision, and perfect everything. It is considered very rude, *like farting in public,* to ask an OT (like church president, Rev. Heber Jentzch) why he wears glasses or reads from a text, since his infallible memory makes this unnecessary.

OTs have access to their past lives and experiences. OTs who have shared these memories report "being run over by a Martian bishop driving a steamroller," and "being transformed into an intergalactic walrus that perished falling out of a flying saucer." *The intergalactic walrus is my personal favorite.*

Music: ★★★ —Many prominent musicians are Scientologists. Although none of them are as yet transparent, I could see right through them. In OT Land, the music is of the spheres, but more than a little off key.

Food: ★ —It's hard to eat when you don't have a body.

Drink: ★ —See food.

Accommodations: ★★ —Spacious and airy, but the vacuum of space was cold and lonely. I wanted some body.

Entry Requirements: ★★ (*The more movie stars the easier the entry*)

OVERALL RATING: ★★

Children of a Jealous God

Ah, women. They make the highs higher and the lows more frequent.
—Friedrich Nietzsche

Notes:
How much does a thetan weigh? "From some experiments conducted about fifteen or twenty years ago—a thetan weighed about 1.5 ounces, or 45 grams! Who made these experiments? Well, a doctor made these experiments."

"I love her," Dirk confided. "But she is hardly what I would describe as an angel ..."

"Well," Lucifer drawled, slowly and deliberately cracking his knuckles, "angels, like gods, aren't exactly what you imagine. There is the chicken and the egg argument. You know—did God create man in His image or vice versa ... and where do women fit in? Well, you're seeing the seedy side of creation. As you know, your God is a jealous God ... well, if that holds true for the Big Guy, just imagine how that trickles down to something as unspecified as guardian angels. I mean, guardian angels aren't exactly angels of great consequence ... like Peter, Gabriel, or ..." Lucifer glanced modestly down at his immaculate hands.

"You have to put yourself in their shoes ... or perhaps ... wings." Lucifer chuckled. "First, they, children of a jealous God, are set the task of 'watching over you.' Then you take up with a cat and—sister or not, cats are noted for their indiscriminate and rather prurient sex habits."

Dirk choked. Not only was Mary his sister ... she was a cat, for Christ's sake: a different species and a tiny, furry one at that.

"I know, I know," replied Lucifer, holding up his hand. "But you must remember that all angels, particularity Angelica, are much less species-specific than you humans. After all, you are, uh ... involved ... with her." The Devil delicately cleared his throat and extended his fingers widely, implying the breadth of involvement. "And you are different species. Then there are the houris."

Lucifer grinned broadly, exhibiting a dazzling show of pearly whites. "No wonder Angelica's jealous; show her some compassion, man."

"She," Dirk replied thoughtfully, "is more envious of you than anyone. She would be the last angel on Earth to defend you."

Lucifer smiled slowly. "Two sides of the same coin."

"What do you mean, 'two sides of the same coin?' What are you trying to tell me?"

Lucifer only smiled maddeningly.

The Decline of Western Civilization

He is one of those people who would be enormously improved by death.
—H. H. Munro (Saki)

It was about this time that strange electrical outages began occurring. Telephone lines went dead, and when they worked, crackled nervously. Blackouts became frequent. Many a shop owner discovered empty spaces on shelves where before had been candy bars, CDs, and other pocketable items. On the other hand, many an armed robbery failed because it is exceedingly difficult to hold a gun to someone's head when you can't see their head. Cell phones frequently died or emitted odd beeping noises. Computers suffered frequent crashes.

Dirk was happily not affected by this, as he was securely connected to the Outernet. Whatever else you might say about Lucifer, his technology was first-rate. Still, Dirk could not open a newspaper or listen to the radio without hearing some irate citizen or concerned columnist bemoaning the decline of Western civilization.

"We are rapidly becoming a Third World country!" raved a popular journalist. "The increasingly frequent blackouts and lack of connections, be they phone, fax, computer, or television, are causing havoc in our fair city. I urge you to rise up and phone, fax, or email your congressman today!"

Although doubtless impassioned, this was a decidedly unfortunate suggestion, as the already-stressed phone, fax, and email lines were immediately overloaded with a surge of fuming phone calls, furious faxes, and enraged emails. The flood of correspondence overtaxed the already-strained system. First everything froze. Then everything died.

There was massive panic.

It took teams of technicians working round several clocks to restart the damaged system. The first words heard on the newly broadcasting radio were from the aforementioned columnist, demanding better service and inciting a call-in campaign.

Later that night, he was felled by an electrical line. The lineman on the scene swore it had been an accident. The lineman was acquitted of any wrongdoing and received a promotion.

Due to the abnormally high rate of blackouts, static, electrical problems, and computer crashes, as well as the normally high rate of wars, plagues, pestilence, and natural disasters, leaders of various denominations began predicting the End of Days with rising frequency. However, due to the normally frequent occurrence of such predictions, only followers of the faith paid any attention.

Angelica grew lovelier with each passing day, but she crackled.

My Fine Lord

I cannot believe in a God who wants to be praised all the time.
—Friedrich Nietzsche

Dirk had just showered and was toweling off. He felt grateful. After his unprepossessing entrance into the Jehovah's Witnesses' afterlife, showering always made him nervous. Actually, many things made Dirk nervous: watering, vacuums, escalators, and anything involving suction action. He never knew where he was going, when he would go, or how he would depart. It was unnerving.

Luckily, the positives in his life counterbalanced the uncertainties. Mary was back. He adored John-John, although he doubted the dog was Angelica's brother. He was a writer and traveler. He feared death no longer, although he doubted it was the best place to spend eternity. True Angelica was a tad difficult. Still, when she wasn't inhaling electricity, trying to asphyxiate him with nail polish, or having fits of jealousy over Mary, John-John, or Lucifer, she was a tonic to his soul.

Humming "Stairway to Heaven," Dirk examined his reflection. He smiled. He was tall and straight. His dark, soulful eyes contained a secret twinkle.

"You handsome devil," he said, raking glossy hair off his forehead with what he hoped was Errol Flynn insouciance.

★

Dirk gave Mary a pat and walked John-John to a dog park. John-John enthusiastically sniffed the hind parts of fellow canines, rolled in mysterious scents, and raced in mad circles. The park was full of grassy discoveries.

John-John bounded up to Dirk, a long curved stick clamped in salivating jaws.

"Want to fetch, boy?" Dirk asked. John-John tossed his head, waggling his tail with such vigor it was a wonder he didn't topple over.

Dirk grabbed the stick. John-John playfully shook his head, anticipating a pre-game tussle. At first Dirk played along, but soon found he was being swung from side to side. With a final heave from John-John, his hands loosened their hold. He was flung up, up, up into blackness.

Dirk awoke in a cross-legged position that was extremely uncomfortable. He had considerable difficulty unfolding his legs from the enforced half-lotus. Rising shakily to his feet, Dirk looked about. He was standing on the edge of a lotus-shaped planet of lush green gardens, purple mountains, and ultramarine streams. Hastily he backed away from the planet's rim, which loomed over a universe of whirling planets.

"Hey, bud, watch where you're walking," a harsh voice snarled. The voice had a Bronx accent. Dirk looked around in confusion,

"Get offa me, you great oaf!" screamed a voice from beneath Dirk's feet. Startled, he jumped backward, closer to the planet's edge.

"Get off me!" a high, thin voice squealed.

Dirk was on Goloka. Here, everything—rocks, leaves, even used tissue paper—contained some of Hare Krishna's spirit.

It was a lovely planet. But it was almost impossible to move there without treading on someone's soul.

DIRK QUIGBY'S GUIDE TO THE HARE KRISHNA AFTERLIFE

The International Society for Krishna Consciousness (ISKCON, or ISaCON) was founded by A. C. Bhaktivedanta Swami Prabhupada in 1966, in New York. It is based on Hindu teachings from the sixteenth century, *a period known for enlightened concepts.*

END DESTINATION:

After death, you enter the womb of your next mother. Which of the 8,400,000 species you will become depends on your consciousness at time of death. If you are in human consciousness, you get a human body. If you are in animal consciousness, you get an animal's body. *If you are in drugged consciousness, you get Keith Richard's body.*

If you have lived a sinful life, you go to a Hellish planet.

If you have been good, you go to a Heavenish one. There are many. You might live ageless and lovely for millions of years, but you're still part of the material world. Eventually you will die and return to Earth.

If you are the best Gaudiya Vaisnava (Krishna devotee) you can be, you ascend to the lotus-shaped Goloka. It's Krishna's hangout, made of transcendental gems, which yield whatever you desire. Here, every word is a song, every step a dance, every moment new, fresh, and exciting.

ENTRY REQUIREMENTS:

God is Krishna, and he is the source of all avatars. Krishna has numerous nicknames, such as Vishnu the Preserver, Jehovah *the vengeful,* Buddha *the fat,* Rama *the blue,* and Allah *the less-said-the-better.* Jesus is an enlightened vegetarian who teaches meditation.

Krishna is perfect! His body is unchanging; he never suffers from overindulgence, *water retention, or irregularity.* He has a glowing complexion the color of rain clouds. He wears peacock feathers in his curly black hair and a flower garland around his neck. *He has a truly super fashion sense and is never misled by the latest fads.* His garments are the color of lightning, and his toenails resemble the light of the moon.

Krishna enjoys himself completely. He is very informal; most of his devotees don't even call him God. If you reach Goloka, there are five ways you can serve Krishna. *Making Krishna's existence perfect appears to be the main goal and function of the universe.*

If you are a neutral devotee, you will enhance Krishna's life by being the best animal, plant, stream, rock, house, or widget you can be. Normally inanimate objects like blow dryers are all fully conscious in Goloka, *although they aren't raconteurs and are rarely invited to dinner parties.*

Service devotees serve as God Fridays.

Fraternal devotees are friends.

Parental devotees act as Krishna's parents. *They help him with his homework and take him to Lotusland, but never enforce curfew or attempt to suppress his sybaritic tendencies.*

Conjugal devotees are *girlfriends, boyfriends, and one-night stands.* "The pure love of God reaches its summit in romantic exchanges with Krishna." *I tried that line at a bar once.*

To get into this very cool place, where even being a piece of used dental floss is fabulous, you must chant, "Hare Krishna, Hare Krishna, Krishna Krishna, Hare Hare, Hare Rama, Hare Rama, Rama Rama, Hare Hare" as often as possible.

It's altruistic to chant publicly, in groups (kirtana parties), allowing all to benefit from the holy names.

Chanting makes you want to follow The Four Principles:

No meat, fish, or eggs.

No intoxication.

No gambling.

No sex. *Krishna is one of those "Do as I say, not do as I do" gods.*

Find an acarya (a guru) who's free of all material desire or sin. He'll give you a mantra which will send you to Goloka. *Unearthing such a guru can be tricky. That's doubtless why so many poor chanters have to repeat that darn birth and rebirth cycle over and over and over again. It can't have to do with those tiny rules about intoxication or sex. Those are easy if you chant.*

Read the *Bhagavad Gita* and *Srimad Bhagavatam*. Reading about Krishna's enjoying sex and his continual partying fills one with desire to reject material things like sex and continual partying.

It is wrong to kill anything, even vegetables. Offer your veggies to Krishna before eating and he will nullify the bad karma. *Except for okra. Krishna hates okra.*

QUALITY RATINGS:
Perks: ★ —You are never at a loss for words; which are: "Hare Krishna, Hare Krishna, Krishna Krishna, Hare Hare, Hare Rama, Hare Rama, Rama Rama, Hare Hare."
Music: ★★ —"Hare Krishna" This award-winning mantra emits powerful energy because for thousands of years Hindus have prayed to God by chanting these names. And Hindus always get their prayers answered.

Okay, if you like house music.
Food: ★★★ —Goloka yields all you desire. I feasted on a very fine facsimile of a beefsteak, almost as good as the real thing.
Drink: ★★★ —See Food.
Accommodations: ★★★ —See Drink.
Entry Requirements: ★★
OVERALL RATING: ★★

Dirk returned five days or fifteen minutes later, vastly relieved that his couch did not object to being sat on. John-John had beaten him home and lay curled up on the doorstep.

Suffer the Little Children ...
and Everyone Else

I've had a wonderful time, but this wasn't it.
—Groucho Marx

Dirk awoke to Mary's gentle kneading. John-John lay contentedly snorting and drooling at his feet. Dirk could not decide whether John-John was the reincarnation of some sweet yet dumb football player, or just a dog.

Angelica was not around. Dirk could usually locate her these days by the scent of smoke or the sizzle of some electrical object relinquishing its unhappy existence. Dirk loved her, but it was more peaceful when she was gone. In addition to her disabling almost every appliance he possessed, her energy was frenetic. Though lovelier and lovelier, she exuded static. Lovemaking was a jolting experience.

Firecrackers were supposed to be felt only briefly during culmination, not throughout the entire copulation.

If Dirk had been watching television instead of quietly lying in bed with his contented companions, he would not have felt nearly so sanguine. But as the TV was usually on the fritz these days, he had gotten out of the habit,

★

Angelica, no longer content with hairdryers and vacuuming swimming pools, had set her sights on bigger bangs and more potent power.

Earlier that day, in a secret location in Crawford, Texas, Killem

Nuclear Weapons Facility was holding an open house. Its managers were hoping to mitigate the fallout from their new plant. This facility had warheads pointing at North Korea, China, Russia, Iran, Iraq, Cuba, and Vermont. The facility's friendly yellow logo glowed brightly, and its motto read: "We're the reason why there's a Glow in the Sky: Killem Nuclear Power—providing safe energy and energetic safety."

As the carefully-monitored crowd of visitors passed through innumerable scanning devices, a beautiful woman with startling gray-green eyes might have been seen joining a tour ... had anyone been watching.

The tour proceeded into the main detonation center.

"This little ol' button here," drawled the virile guard, eyes as blue and vacant as the Texas sky, "holds the power to destroy and is therefore our protection against—"

Before you could say "Defcon 7," the aforementioned beautiful woman detached herself from the crowd, and with superhuman strength flung herself on the guard. She hurled him to the ground and tore out his windpipe. This proved an impediment to the continuation of his painstakingly memorized recitation..

As the crowd screamed, a host of armed guards rounded on the woman, opening fire.

The woman (whom we might as well call Angelica, for it was she) leaped over the guard's prone body to the control panels, where she rapidly punched buttons in coded sequence. She appeared impervious to the bullets that flew about and even through her.

One of the guards whipped out his cell phone and frantically dialed a double-secret, top-private number.

It rang directly into the presidential suite.

The president was in, happily practicing shots with his newly purchased Tiger Woods putter.

Absently he picked up the phone.

"Sir," choked out a terrified voice, "the GZ Phukital sequence has been activated—"

"Hole-in-one," the president chortled.

By an unfortunate coincidence, "hole-in-one" was the exact phrase necessary to provide presidential approval for an all-out nuclear strike.

"Oh, well, sir," the guard sighed, a hint of a sob evident in his muted tones, "I guess I'll hang up now. Want to say 'good-bye' to the wife and kids."

"Hole-in-one!" the president repeated gleefully.

All over the globe, shocked masses and their horrified leaders gazed up at the sky.

The last vision, ineffably burned into their retinas as their shadows were soon to be burned into the ground, was of a blazing mass hurtling towards them with the burning glory of a falling star, containing within it the inevitability of death, and the unspoken promise that they would never have to pay taxes again.

The last action taken by the leaders of North Korea, China, Russia, Iran, Iraq, and Cuba was to hit in their detonation codes. And as the leaders of Germany, England, France, Pakistan, Israel, and India watched the crisscrossing missiles overhead, they too flipped their ignition switches. They absolutely refused to become the only remaining taxpayers on the face of the planet!

The governor of Vermont was out tapping maple syrup and, as usual, remained blissfully oblivious to the madness and destruction rising about him.

Dirk Quigby's Guide
to the Afterlife

We will all burn together when we burn
There will be no need to stand and wait your turn
When it's time for the fall-out
And Saint Peter calls us all out
We'll just drop our agendas and adjourn.
—Tom Lehrer

It was late. Dirk was tired. As he climbed into bed, he heard a knock on his door. It was Lucifer. Dirk realized that he had missed his deadline for "Hare Krishna." Before he could begin to try to think up an excuse, Lucifer held up his hand.

"Don't worry about it. It really doesn't matter anymore. I just came by to let you know that there's no hurry."

"No hurry? What do you mean?" Dirk asked. "Surely there are more Paradises to preview?"

"Oh," Lucifer waved his hand vaguely, "there are endless afterlives. It's just that I'm going to be rather busy for a bit ... So—no rush and no worries."

He punched Dirk affectionately on the arm and turned to go.

"Wait," Dirk cried. "Have you seen Angelica lately?" Although Lucifer and Angelica weren't exactly friends ... Lucifer knew everyone. He was a social Devil. If anyone had seen her ...

"Can't say ... exactly," Lucifer replied. "But one thing's for sure, she's going to be very busy too."

Before Dirk could ask what he meant by "exactly," Lucifer vanished.

Dirk lay in bed. Mary's purring and John-John's snoring soothing him. He was an otherworldly traveler, chronicling diverse heavens and mysterious ghouls. He was building bridges with words and fostering understanding with his pen.

His girlfriend, though not angelic, was an angel.

He was encased by the unconditional, furry love of Mary and John-John.

"I have been bombed three times," Dirk cooed softly, petting the purring cat. "I must be immortal."

Outside rose a noise too vast to be heard, the calm before a waterfall, the silence before a tsunami. In the quiet dawn a dozen faint lines of smoke rose, blossoming like gray flowers into huge mushrooms shapes.

Angelica had finally found her ultimate fix.

★

The air was a tangle of souls, souls heading toward purgatory, toward judgment, to Heaven or Hell.

Dirk, or rather Dirk's soul, said a prayer for the next world that had Angelica as its guardian angel.

He looked at the confusion of ghosts curling about him.

Once again I've been writing copy for a product that's gone out of business.

Peering more closely at the writhing masses, Dirk saw in each transparent hand a translucent copy of *Dirk Quigby's Guide to the Afterlife*.

Some spirits were noticeably ashen, even for haunts. These superlucent beings flipped through pages with frantic haste. Every now and again, one would vanish with a soft "pop," leaving behind a clear, slightly moist, copy of the *Guide*, drifting in space.

So much for the atheists.

Others had already marked their destination and were hurriedly reviewing requirements.

Who would have thought the judgment bar would be like this? No one was standing in line, waiting for an angry God to propel him to Heaven or to Hell.

No, instead, ghosts streamed through the air, perusing their guidebooks.

Dirk smiled. He would never win a Pulitzer, as the Pulitzer committee now consisted of a few black shadows scorched onto the earth. But he had, without a doubt, written the ultimate guidebook.

Turning, Dirk noticed a cloud podium. Behind it floated a darkly handsome gentleman, roll book in hand.

God looked oddly familiar; something about the way he examined his nails.

Dirk contemplated offering autographs, but wasn't certain he could hold a pen.

Acknowledgments

I'd like to thank the friends who read early versions of Dirk and encouraged me, among them: Melanie Stephens, Sierra Silverstone, Katherine Huber, Marie Spenle, Dave Collins, Gillian Caballero Chase, Lesley Moussette, John Eichinger, Sir Brian of Biscuit (Brian Lister) Brian Agincourt Massey, the diverse, giving Jill Catherine and more ... but the book's supposed to be fewer than 70,000 words.

Fanatical gratitude to Zoran Ivančić, for facts
and friendship—forever,

Ray Bradbury for support and love,

Mike Madrid for fabulous book design,
Brian Griffith for conscientious copy editing,
and Nate Dorward for perfect typesetting,

and my Fabulous Publisher/Editor/Friend
and all around Supergirl Tod Davies.

Thanks to EAP, giving voice to new ideas
and ways of seeing.

Bibliography of Books and Websites

BOOKS:

Ashton, John, and Tom Whyte. *The Quest for Paradise: Visions of Heaven and Eternity in the World's Myths and Religions.* New York: Harper Collins, 2001.

Editors of Larousse. *Religions of the World.* Lincolnwood, IL: NTC/Contemporary Publishing Group, Inc., Peter Bedrick Books, 2002.

Eliade, Mircea and Ioan P. Couliano, with Hillary S. Wiesner. *The Harper Collins Concise Guide to World Religions.* New York: Harper Collins Publishers, 1991.

Fisher, Mary Pat. *Living Religions.* Fourth edition. Upper Saddle River, N.J.: Prentice-Hall, 1999.

Johnson, Christopher, Jay, PhD and Marsha G. McGee, PhD. *How Different Religions View Death and Afterlife.* Second edition. Philadelphia: The Charles Press, 1998.

Judson, Olivia. *Dr. Tatiana's Sex Advice to All Creation.* New York: Metropolitan Books, 2002.

Langley, Myrtle. *Religion (Eyewitness Books).* New York: Alfred A. Knopf, 1996.

McCasland, S. Vernon, Grace E. Cairns, and David C. Yu. *Religions of the World.* New York: Random House, 1969.

Muhammad, Elijah. *The True History of Jesus as Taught by the Honorable Elijah Muhammad.* Chicago: Coalition for the Remembrance of Elijah, 1992.

Renard, John. *The Handy Religion Answer Book.* Canton, MI: Visible Ink Press, 2002.

Roberts, Arthur O. *A Quaker Perspective.* Philadelphia: The Charles Press, 1998.

Stebbins, Robert C. *A Field Guide to Western Reptiles and Amphibians (Peterson Field Guide Series).* Boston: Houghton Mifflin Company, 1966.

Wallace, Robert A. *How They Do It.* New York: William Morrow and Company, 1980.

Wilkinson, Philip. *Illustrated Dictionary of Religions.* New York: Dorling Kinderling Limited, London, 1999.

Also, the Bhagavad Gita, the Bible, the Book of Mormon, the Holy Qur'an, and The Torah.

A Very Few Websites:

In addition to the sites below, I used hundreds of others, always including one or more official Church websites.

Bible charts, fairly accurate but Christian: http://www.rose-publishing.com

Born Again sites

http://www.godhatesfags.com/ —need I say more?
http://www.raptureready.com/rap2.html
From the raptureready webmaster: "I have no master plan for maintaining Rapture Ready all the way through the seven-year tribulation. After the big event takes place, I expect RR to last several months. After all, the internet was designed to survive a nuclear war. It should be able to survive the great catching up of all believers."

Everything sites: http://en.wikipedia.org/

Mormon sites

Mormon nephites. A really, really funny "Official Nephite sighting Center": http://nowscape.com/mormon/3nephites.htm

"So what's your experience with the nephites?": http://www.freerepublic.com/focus/religion/2343118/posts

The God makers: http://www.archive.org/details/God_Makers
Temple rituals: http://video.google.com/videoplay?docid=6551397027295071865
A reenactment of temple ritual is shown, which is said to be performed for the purpose of "evangelizing the dead." "Several people discuss 'holy Mormon underwear,' and several stories are told of people who refused to remove this underwear under any circumstances, including bathing and giving birth."

A pretty funny *South Park* about Mormons: http://www.southparkstudios.com/guide/712/

Scientology sites

Tom Cruise on Scientology. Wacky but cute: http://www.youtube.com/watch?v=UFBZ_uAbxSo

Scientology: Shut Up in the Name of Thetans. A film on copywriter and scientology (ex. and current members talk): http://www.youtube.com/watch?v=F9-wgwtCcnQ

"The Scandal of Scientology." Contains "real" past-life memories: www.clambake.org/archive/books/tsos/sos-04.html

Dr. Carbone—International Association of Past Life Therapists: http://www.pastlifememories.net/

Unification Church sites

Very interesting book/video/website about Mr. Moon: *King of America*, by John Goronfeld: http://www.gorenfeld.net/book/

"In 2004, author John Gorenfeld scooped the Washington press corps when he exposed a creepy dinner party on Capitol Hill. With lawmakers participating, the Times publisher held a ritual coronation for himself as the 'King of Peace.' Wearing a majestic cape and coronet, he declared himself Messiah. The New York Times editors compared the event, sponsored by a U.S. senator, to an act of the Roman emperor Caligula."

Jon Stewart on Mr. Moon: http://www.thedailyshow.com/watch/wed-june-30-2004/moon-units

E. E. King has been a ballet dancer, actor, comic,
teacher, artist, biologist, horticulturalist,
mushroom hunter, free diver,
art & science director,
and wild animal rehabilitator.

She has painted, taught, danced,
looked for frogs and acted (badly)
in Spain, Bosnia, Italy, London, Korea,
L.A., San Francisco,
Puerto Rico and Mexico.

She has won various awards, but is far too modest
to mention them here.

She was raised in a household
that doesn't force religion on kids.
This book is the result.

★